"That's better than sex."

Dusty tried not to grin. "Depends on who you've been doing it with," he replied in an indolent drawl. "Personally, I don't think it comes close. But that's just me."

Her grin was cocky, and bypassing the chair across from the desk, she slid up onto the desk top itself. "So you're saying that sex with you is more exciting than a power dive from a thousand to six feet in ten seconds."

He leaned back in his chair, propped his feet on the edge of the desk and crossed his arms behind his head. "You sound pretty curious. Wanna find out?"

She gave him a look that only men were supposed to give. "Can you take me to places I've never been before?" she asked seductively.

He grinned. "If I do, there's no going home again...."

ABOUT THE AUTHOR

Tracy Hughes began writing her first romance novel
after graduating from Northeast Louisiana University
in 1984. While in graduate school, she finished that
book in lieu of her thesis and decided to abandon her
pursuit of a master's degree and follow her dream of
becoming a writer. She is the award-winning author of
over a score of novels, including two mainstream titles
and a historical romance. Tracy recently relocated to
Mississippi with her husband and children.

Books by Tracy Hughes

HARLEQUIN AMERICAN ROMANCE

381–HONORBOUND
410–SECOND CHANCES
438–FATHER KNOWS BEST
455–SAND MAN

HARLEQUIN SUPERROMANCE

304–ABOVE THE CLOUDS
342–JO: CALLOWAY CORNERS, BOOK 2
381–EMERALD WINDOWS
399–WHITE LIES AND ALIBIS

TRACY HUGHES

DELTA DUST

Harlequin Books

TORONTO • NEW YORK • LONDON
AMSTERDAM • PARIS • SYDNEY • HAMBURG
STOCKHOLM • ATHENS • TOKYO • MILAN
MADRID • WARSAW • BUDAPEST • AUCKLAND

For my husband, Ken, who freed my spirit.

Special thanks to Ellis Warren, of Ellis Warren
Flying Service in Benton, Mississippi, for his
crop-dusting expertise.

Published September 1993

ISBN 0-373-16502-1

DELTA DUST

Chapter One

The next best thing to a nosedive from twenty thousand feet was the weightless leap of her Porsche after topping a hill at ninety miles per hour. Cindy Hartzell rammed her foot on the accelerator, trying for a clean ninety-five down Highway 16 as the wind ripped over her windshield. It was funny how the air always smelled the same at home, whether you were tearing down the road in a car or splitting the clouds in a jet. It all smelled like Mississippi cotton fields, knee-high rows of beans and fertile delta sand.

Carelessly navigating her way down the curving road, she reached up and freed the clasp from her hair, letting the wind whip through it. Blond streams of silky hair flapped over the headrest as she turned her face up to the sun.

Above her, she saw a crop duster, making a last cloudy ascent from a field a mile away, and smiling, she waved. He tipped a wing in response, and she knew he was watching her as he curved around the field and flew toward her from behind.

A mischievous thrill rose inside her as the plane circled her car, and punching the pedal, she urged the Porsche even faster, over a hundred miles per hour. The wind grew hot against her face, and looking for relief, she began unbuttoning her shirt.

The plane flew ahead of her, and she waved goodbye, maneuvering the wheel with her knee as she finished opening her shirt to reveal the bikini top she wore beneath it, just in case an ideal burst of tanning rays presented itself. Slipping her shirt off her shoulders, she pulled it off her arms.

She heard the plane engine roar behind her and glanced back to see the crop duster dropping down to buzz a few feet above her head. She swerved, then recovered instantly. Grinning, she lifted her shirt and waved it at him like a surrendering flag.

The plane tilted to the left and swooped out of sight, and she laughed aloud again. This was going to be the best move she'd ever made, she told herself. It was time somebody put some fun back into life in Yazoo City.

But more importantly, it was time for Yazoo City to put some life back into her fun.

DUSTY WEBB CIRCLED his air tractor back around and found the convertible again, with the half-naked blonde flying through the county like an image out of one of his dreams. He laughed aloud and shook his head, wondering if he had enough fuel just to follow her until she stopped somewhere. He'd gladly put the plane down in a tree or a parking lot...it didn't really matter. It wasn't every day that he ran across a prize like this while spraying crops.

And what a flirt she was, he thought, grinning as he watched her wave her shirt up at him, just daring him to do something about it. He groaned slightly at the challenge and circled the area again.

Up ahead at two o'clock, his hangar came into view, and he checked his fuel gauge again. There wasn't time to follow her. He needed to refuel and refill his hopper, then defoliate the Stockstill field on the other side of the mill.

Deciding on one last circle, he cut his plane to the right and arced back behind her. But before he could dip and buzz her, she made a quick right turn, forcing the car into a screech that almost started a power spin. Laughing, she recovered immediately and left two stripes of burned rubber in her wake.

Damn, he thought. She must be going 110. If a patrolman came by, he'd probably throw her in jail. That is, after he took a good look at what that bikini top covered, then made a quick frisk of those skimpy little shorts she wore, just to make sure she wasn't hiding any weapons.

He laughed, thinking that her weapons were already well exposed, and wondered if she used them as well as she flaunted them. Again, he groaned, then turned his plane toward home.

Her car turned onto the dirt road leading to his hangar, and as he circled his strip to land, he watched her tearing toward him.

How had she known he'd be landing here? he asked himself, but quickly he dismissed the question and decided to count his blessings that she had. It was a fantasy come true, he thought as he started his descent and saw her getting out of her car. This amazing blonde on *his* doorstep. The blonde with the bikini top...and the tiny little shorts...and the tanned legs...

His plane jolted him at touchdown, and he shook himself, remembering that he couldn't afford another accident. He still hadn't paid for the last one yet.

He cut his speed, put on his brakes and rolled from the dirt strip onto the concrete.

As he grew closer, the woman leaned back against the hood of her car. She had put her shirt back on, but it hung unbuttoned over her bikini top. He wondered if she wore the bottom of the suit beneath her shorts, or lacy panties, or perhaps nothing at all....

He turned the plane around, righting it for reloading and refueling, then cut off the engine and opened the cockpit door. Tearing off his helmet, he got out, stepped onto the wing, and jumped onto the concrete.

"I should have known it was you," the woman said with a grin that suggested she knew something he didn't.

Dusty straightened up, raked a hand through his hair and strode toward her. "Do I know you?"

"Sure you do," she said. "I was the woman in the car you were showing off for."

He grinned. "I know that. You said you should have known it was me."

"Dusty, right?" she asked. "Dusty Webb?"

His eyes narrowed in confusion. "Well...yeah. Were you looking for me?"

"I was looking *at* you," she said. "You're a pretty good pilot."

"Pretty good?" he repeated, chuckling.

"And I noticed you were looking at me, too. You almost hit a telephone pole. Is that why you crashed before? Because you were watching a woman?"

Dusty's grin faded instantly. "You obviously wanted me to watch you or you wouldn't have been driving a hundred miles an hour and waving your clothes around like a banner."

She threw her head back and laughed, and one hand came up to shake out the hair streaming around her shoulders as if it hadn't just been mercilessly wind-blown. "I always drive fast. And I like the sun."

He shook his head at her disjointed response and glanced down at the bikini top he had so admired from his plane. His grin inched back across his face. "You put your shirt back on."

She knew the power she had over him, he thought with a twist of discomfort.

"Yeah. I always try to dress appropriately when I conduct business."

The fissure between his brows deepened. "What kind of business?"

At that, she thrust out her hand—a small hand with short-cut nails—and took his. "I'm Cindy Hartzell," she said.

He felt the blood draining from his face as the reality slowly sank in. "Cindy Hartzell? The one who—?"

"That's right," she said with a delighted smile. "The one who just bought your business. Looks like I'm your new boss."

Chapter Two

"My new boss?" Dusty Webb took a step back and looked at her with new eyes. "Wait a minute. They said this was a tax shelter. That you were out of the country or something."

Cindy laughed and started toward the yellow plane he'd just gotten out of. "I didn't tell anyone I was coming home. I wanted to surprise my family."

Following a few steps behind her, he gaped at her. "What about me? Did you want to surprise me, too?"

Her grin was unwavering as she looked back at him. "Well, from the looks of you, I'd say you are." She bent down and checked one of the nozzles on the spreader that ran the length of the wing.

Dusty shook his head. "No. This can't be happening. Your lawyer led me to believe that you were in Australia or somewhere. That I'd probably never even see you...."

Cindy looked up. "Is that what he said?"

"Well...not in so many words...but everybody knows you haven't been in Yazoo City in years."

"So you assumed that I'd just hand over the money to bail you out of trouble, just out of the kindness of my heart, huh?"

"Well, no, of course not. I thought it was a tax shelter."

"And did my attorney tell you that?"

"No," he said again.

"You just assumed." She nodded and, patting the fuselage as if the plane were an old friend, she left it and went to the big holding tanks on the edge of the runway, where chemicals were mixed. "Would have been pretty convenient, wouldn't it?" she asked as she examined the hoses. "I bail you out and then never show my face around here to interfere."

"Hey, he told me I could still run the business. I *know* he told me that."

Satisfied with the condition of the tanks and the open shed sheltering them, she started toward the hangar. "The contract says that you can continue working here. In fact, I want you to stay on as chief pilot."

"Well, that's just great," Dusty spouted, "considering I'm the only pilot around."

"Not anymore," she said. "I'm going to be flying the second plane."

"You're *what?*" The words came out more obstinately than he'd planned, but she didn't stop to answer him. She was through the front door before he shouted, "Wait a minute. Do you even have a license?"

"Of course I do," she said. "A commercial one. I've been flying for years."

He let that information soak in for a moment, then shook his head and followed her into the office area of the building. "All right, so you can fly. Have you ever worked as an aerial applicator?"

"You mean a crop duster?" Smiling, she checked out the small waiting area where farmers could shoot the breeze and drink coffee on slow days. "No, but I spent the last six weeks training at the agricultural pilots' school in Atlanta. I'm still green, but with a little practice—"

He shook his head. "No way. This is not what I agreed to."

She turned back to him. "You agreed to sell me your business, and I agreed to buy it. That means I'm in charge, Dusty, and you work for me."

"But you weren't supposed to show up!" he shouted. "You were supposed to write me a check from some nice clean little desk down under, collect the rest of the profits and keep your nose out of it! That's the way your family does it!"

Cindy considered that for a moment, then shook her head. "You may have heard, I don't exactly fit into my family's mold."

"Oh boy, have I heard." Turning away, he went into his office, and she followed him. "You're the black sheep of the family. The one who flounces all over the world collecting troubles like, no doubt, you collect men." He slammed his helmet down on his desk and spun back around to her. The laughter in her eyes was maddening.

"I don't know about that last part, although I suppose I have gotten into my share of trouble." She shrugged. "But I'm home now. And I've got to make a living. We have two planes, and—"

"*I* have two planes!" he shouted.

"No, *I* have two planes, if you want to get that technical. You sold me your business, Dusty. My understanding is that you had debts up to your ears and were looking at bankruptcy. I bailed you out, and now, if it's the last thing I do, I'm going to get this business back on its feet. It's a mess, and it's going to take a lot of work, but I know I can do it."

Dusty dropped into the chair behind his desk and raked his hand through his raven hair again. His face was tanned from all the hours in the cockpit, and his biceps swelled from fighting the g-forces as he did his aerial acrobatics as easily as others parallel-parked. "If my business is a mess, it's because I was laid up for a year. I couldn't work, so I couldn't pay my plane notes, and I owe on the hangar. My other two pilots left and started a competing business down the road. Stole all my farmers right out from under me."

Cindy smiled and perched on the arm of a chair across from his desk. "Well, if you don't mind my saying so, you sure have healed well."

He gave her a contemplative look, as if he didn't know whether her words were complimentary or not. Her shirt still hung unbuttoned, and his eyes inadvertently dropped to her breasts, then darted away.

"Yeah, well the business didn't. I've gotten back a good many of my farmers, but not enough to get me out of debt."

"Then aren't you glad I came along? I have a great head for business, believe it or not. It's probably inbred. My family owns half the county, you know. And I have a real talent for persuasion. I'll bet I can win back all the farmers you lost."

"How? By taking off your shirt and waving it in their faces?" He chuckled without feeling, then shrugged. "Come to think of it, it would probably work."

She grinned. "I won't need to take my shirt off, thank you. I've known most of the farmers since I was born."

He shook his head as if he couldn't believe her naïveté and got up to come around his desk. All six feet two inches of him towered above her, and she smiled at the blue in his eyes that belied his tough facade. "You just don't get it, do you, honey?" he asked. "These farmers don't want some cute little blonde spraying their crops. They want a professional. Their livelihood depends on it."

"I am a professional, and I'm a darn good pilot."

He breathed a disbelieving laugh. "You've got to be kidding. I've been flying for fifteen years, and I still have close calls all the time. You can't just come in here and start spraying fields like you know what you're doing. You won't make it through the first day."

"I'm not afraid of danger."

"I saw that when you were flying down the road," he said. "But you've never known danger like this kind of danger. Stupidity and recklessness don't pay off in this business! You have a death wish? Go bungy jumping or something."

"Do you have a death wish?" she flung back.

"We're talking about you."

"No. We're talking about the myth of the ag-pilot. Everybody knows you all have death wishes."

"If I had, I wouldn't have fought so hard to stay alive after the accident."

"I heard," she said. "You were in the hospital, in and out of a coma, for weeks afterward. Would have been easy just to slip out, wouldn't it? But you didn't, because contrary to popular opinion, you *don't* have a death wish. Just like I don't. The truth, Dusty, is that I have a *life* wish. I like living a life that busts at the seams. I like feeling things with every sense I have. I like excitement and adrenaline and the rush you get every time you take off. The bottom line is that boredom is intolerable to me. That's why I want to be a crop duster."

He didn't quite know how to answer her. He'd had those same feelings himself. Now, as he stood looking at her, with her blue eyes so full of passion about something he cared fiercely about as well, he wondered if he should just throw in the towel altogether and hire on in Idaho spraying potatoes. Handing the business he'd raised from scratch over to some fly-by-night Hartzell who had blown in on a whim was a little more than he could bear, but the thought of working beside her every day, watching that little body prance and tease him . . .

"This won't work, Cindy. You might as well know that right now."

"No wonder your business is dying. With that attitude, I'm surprised you didn't just burn the place down."

"We're not talking about my teaching you to file. We're talking about a life-or-death proposition. Crop-dusting is more dangerous than anything you've ever done."

"I can do it," she said. "Trust me."

"But you've never been known to sit still for more than a few months. If you were to start spraying, and if you did get all my farmers back, you couldn't just up and leave whenever you started getting bored. Those people would depend on you. When they call you at six on a Sunday morning, you've got to go. A day's delay can destroy a crop. What am I gonna do when July comes and you get sick of the long hot hours and start wishing you were back in Australia?"

"It won't happen. I'm here to stay."

"Yazoo City, Mississippi, isn't exactly the hot spot of the world. What on earth makes you think you'll be happy here?"

"It's my home," she said, a reluctant vulnerability suddenly invading her tone. "It's where I grew up. It's where my family is."

"But you left to get away from all that."

She smiled. "You have done your homework, haven't you?" She stopped and sighed, then plopped into a chair and pulled her leg up to rest her chin on her knee. "Yeah, I left to get away from all that, but I guess all my travels have taught me where I really need to be."

"Then be here," he said. "Move back into your parents' mansion, let their servants wait on you, get active in the Junior League . . . but don't come in here and try to take over something you know absolutely nothing about."

Cindy's face hardened. "I know more than you think. And your picture of my family isn't quite realistic. I'm not exactly being welcomed back with open arms. I have some things to prove to them. Some mistakes to make up for. This is the way I'm gonna do it."

"And while you're doing it, you'll be screwing up my business."

"It's not your business anymore. It's mine."

"But I've built it up for years. This hangar—I built it with my bare hands. I hammered in every nail. I hung the engine on both of those planes myself. I've been a vital part of the yield of every farm in this area for the last fifteen years. . . ."

"That's why I want you to keep flying for me. But face it, Dusty. If I hadn't come along, you'd have been auctioning those planes off, along with the hangar and the land. No one told you you'd get a free ride from me. If there's anything I've learned in the past few years, it's that there *are* no free rides." She brought her leg down, distracting him, and came to her feet. "Now, the way I see it, you can stay here, and we'll keep your name on the sign out front. Everybody knows this as Webb's Flying Service, and I see no point in changing it. Or, you can leave and go work for someone else, flying someone else's plane and dusting someone else's customers' crops. It wouldn't be hard for me to find another pilot. It's up to you.''

Expelling a heavy, exasperated breath, he dropped down onto the edge of his desk and rubbed his hand through his dark hair. The thought of going to work somewhere else almost made him ill. At least if he stayed here he could see that his planes were cared for, could continue the upkeep on the hangar, could keep things running smoothly... though it shouldn't matter to him one way or another since it would never be his again.

He watched her as she strolled to the shelves on his wall, checking out the vintage-model crop dusters he kept, along with the black-and-white framed photos of his father, one of the state's crop-dusting pioneers, standing in front of his plane. She bent over to examine the propeller, one of the few pieces of his father's plane he'd been able to salvage after the old man's fatal crash.

Had she bought all the memories, too? he wondered bitterly. Or was he at least allowed to keep those?

She touched one of the blades, then turned back to him. ''Is this one of your props?''

''No,'' he said. ''It was my father's. It was intact after his crash, so I kept it.''

She straightened, and her eyes changed. ''I'm sorry. Was he killed?''

"Yep. About twelve years ago. Died doing what he loved best."

"It must have been hard for you," she said, touching the prop again. "Did you have trouble flying after that?"

"A little," he said, "but then I remembered my father's love of it, and all he'd taught me, and I realized that if my time's gonna come, it's gonna come. It did make me careful, though."

He lost his train of thought as she bent over and looked at the books he had on his bottom shelf. His eyes moved from the propeller, back to her little rump, encased in those sexy-as-hell cutoffs, and suddenly he realized things could be worse.

"If I were to stay," he said with a ragged sigh, "there would have to be a few conditions attached. Number one, you don't interfere in the care of those planes. No one knows them like I do. I call the shots in their upkeep."

"Roger that," she said with a cocky smile as she stood up.

Her flip answer riled him more, and he compressed his lips and stared at her. "The second thing is that you dress appropriately. No more bikini tops and cutoff jeans."

Her smile crept farther across her face. "Distracting you, is it?"

He didn't like admitting it, but he feared there was no way to hide it. "Yeah, a little. When I'm flying, I need to concentrate."

"Of course you do," she said. "And so do I. So I suppose you should stop wearing those tight little tank tops."

Dusty looked down at the tank top he wore. "I always wear these. It gets hot, getting in and out of the plane all the time."

She smiled. "I get hot, too, Dusty."

The double meaning stopped him dead for a moment, and he couldn't help the slow grin coming to his lips. "I'll just bet you do."

"I meant when I'm flying," she said, that grin never faltering. "I like dressing cool. And frankly, I'd hate it if you stopped wearing those shirts. You have a great chest, you know."

He felt the blood rushing to places he'd rather it didn't rush just now, and he took a step toward her and met her eyes. "I was just thinking the same thing about you."

She looked up at him, not the least bit intimidated by his size or his boldness. "Sure you want me to cover up?"

"At work, yes," he said.

"And at play?" Her grin could have landed a sane man in a padded cell.

"We'll see."

"No, we won't," she said. "That's my condition. This relationship will never work if we get involved. Sex has to stay out of it."

His voice dropped a decibel as he looked boldly down at the swell of her breasts. "Come on. There has to be an up side to this relationship, as you call it. Besides, you don't exactly come across as someone who isn't interested.''

"Oh, I'm interested," she admitted, lifting her chin and locking into his eyes. "No question about that. But I'm also pretty determined about making this work. I think we'll just have to settle for fantasizing about each other. I can live with that. Can you?''

He narrowed his eyes and gazed dubiously down at her, and that agitation crept back into his subconscious. "Sure," he said. "That won't be hard. But I'll wear whatever I damn well please to work."

She nodded. "Me too, then.''

His face reddened as she strolled out of the office and perused the open hangar, where one of the planes was still parked. Tools hung neatly along the walls, and Dusty's truck sat in the place where the other plane would be put to bed later. "You keep a nice hangar," she said, going toward the plane and giving it a once-over. "And clean planes. I think I've made a good decision here." She started through the open doors of the hangar onto the tarmac toward her car, and his eyes dropped to her small denim-encased hips as he followed. When she reached her Porsche, she turned around. "I'll be here at six-thirty tomorrow morning, Dusty, all revved up and ready to dig in. See you then.''

He set his hands on his hips and tried to concentrate on being agitated again, but somehow it couldn't compete with the thrill rising inside him as she hopped into the driver's seat, threw the car into gear and shot out onto the road again.

THE HOMEPLACE STILL looked the same as Cindy turned onto the long drive that led to the house. Some things never changed, she thought, and for that, she should thank God. But sometimes things did change. People changed. She supposed it would take an awful lot of effort to convince her parents that it could happen to her.

She pulled her car to a stop out in front of the house where company always parked, and sat for a moment, absorbing the sounds of birds chirping in the trees around her, the smell of just-mowed grass wafting across the lawn, the whisper of the leaves in the oak tree she used to climb when she was a child. A smile was conceived in the deepest part of her, then made its way to her lips. How could she have ever hated it so? How could she have wanted so badly to run away and never look back?

She left her bag in the back seat of the car, not certain whether she'd be invited to stay, and made her way up the steps to the front door. Her parents had taken her key away years ago, when they'd told her how disappointed they were in her irresponsibility, and indicated that they couldn't trust her with so simple a thing as a key. It was their way of disowning her, she knew, their way of telling her she had been dismissed as a member of the family.

And all over money.

But she couldn't blame them. It had been irresponsible to take her trust fund and blow it flitting around the world, then come home and ask them for more. It had been irresponsible to get linked up in the press with a member of the royal family, even if their friendship had been strictly platonic. Her parents hadn't known that.

And she supposed she hadn't helped matters any when her brothers had flown to Sweden to talk her into coming home and settling down, and found her working in a casino by night so that she could afford her flying lessons during the day. They had demanded that she come home immediately and they'd forget everything they'd seen, but she had proudly told them that she was earning an honest living and was having fun—the most important element in her life—and that they could be on their way if they had a problem with it.

And then there had been the marriage. Her parents had tried with all their might to talk her out of marrying the Can-Am racer, but she had done it, anyway. The whole family had turned out for the wedding, which took place in Ontario, and despite their disapproval of the groom, who had skipped out of the reception and disappeared for hours, they had tried to give her their blessings.

But worse than the marriage, she supposed, was the divorce. After discovering her husband was sleeping with her best friend, she had left him. Her family had warned her via telephone that divorce was not an acceptable option in their family. She had made her bed, now she must sleep in it. She promptly informed them that beds weren't just for sleeping, and she'd do whatever she jolly well pleased in hers.

It was on her next visit home that her parents washed their hands of her, and she supposed she had pushed them to that point.

She rang the bell, fidgeting slightly as she heard someone attempting to open the door. When the door finally opened, an old woman was peering up at Cindy. "Yes?"

"Hi, Ouida. How are you?"

The woman looked up at her, trying to place her, but Cindy could see that there was no recognition. "It's me, Ouida. Cindy."

"Cindy? No, hon. She ain't here."

"No, Ouida. *I'm* Cindy. It's been a few years, but it's me."

"Livin' in Austria," the old woman said. "Never see her no more."

"Australia," Cindy said, raising her voice. "I lived in Australia. And it's me, Ouida. I'm home."

Just as a tiny glimmer of recognition passed over the old woman's cataractous eyes, Cindy heard someone coming through the foyer from the kitchen. She looked behind Ouida and saw her mother.

Ellen Hartzell gasped at the sight of her daughter, and for a split second, Cindy was sure she saw a smile in her eyes. But just as quickly, it vanished, and that coolness passed over her again. "What are you doing here?"

Cindy wilted. "Oh, Mama. Don't I even get a hug?"

The woman seemed unable to deny her daughter that, and when Cindy threw her arms around her neck, she felt an infinitesimal squeeze in return. "Ouida didn't recognize me, did you, Ouida?"

Ouida strained to see her more clearly, until finally she asked, "Cindy? That you?"

"It's me, Ouida," Cindy said, embracing the old woman as well. "Oh, it's so good to be home."

She released the woman and turned back to her mother, who still stood stoically watching her. "I'm home to stay, Mama," she said. "And I don't plan on ever leaving Yazoo County again."

Her mother only looked at her with sad, disbelieving eyes, then quietly turned and went into the kitchen.

Chapter Three

Cindy tried to tell herself that her mother's reception was cool only because she was busy packing picnic baskets in the kitchen. It didn't matter that she hadn't seen her daughter in two years. People were waiting.

Quietly, Cindy grabbed a spoon and began making tuna finger sandwiches as her mother stirred the tea. "Where's the picnic?" she asked.

"On the church grounds," her mother answered. "Your father and brothers are already there."

"So they left you to do all the work?"

Ellen shook her head. "This is what I do, Cindy. I enjoy it."

"Then how come you look so upset?"

Her mother stopped stirring and looked her fully in the eye. "Because I wasn't expecting you."

"And I've thrown a wrench in your plans."

Ellen set the spoon down and popped the top on the Tupperware pitcher. "That's not the point, Cindy. It's just like you to fly in without a word. Couldn't you have told someone you were coming?"

"Would you have been happy?" Cindy asked. "Would you have looked forward to it? Or would you have just built up some kind of dread, wondering what I'm going to dump on you this time?"

"Well..." her mother said. "What *are* you going to dump on us? Might as well get it right out."

Cindy didn't know why her mother's response hurt her so. After all, she had said it first. And rightfully so. She had always managed to bring home some earth-shattering news... as if she felt it her obligation to breathe some excitement into her mundane family. "Well...I don't have AIDS, Mom, and I'm not pregnant, and there aren't any porn movies coming out with my name on them..."

"You see?" Ellen said, spinning around to her. "That's just the kind of thing I'm talking about. Your sarcasm. Do you think I enjoy being talked to that way by my own daughter?"

"I'm not talking to you 'that way,'" she said on a sigh. "I just thought I'd get your worst fears out of the way so we could get on with this."

"I assure you I haven't lain awake nights worrying about you being in porn films. In fact, the thought never occurred to me until now. But thank you for reminding me that there are still frontiers you haven't explored. Sometimes it's hard to imagine."

Quiet settled over them as Cindy finished the sandwiches. She looked up when she'd run out of bread, and saw her mother putting brownies into a box. Her mother had always made the best picnics, she thought.

And now, with all the grandchildren, she supposed it was one of her mother's favorite things.

The fact that it hadn't been her own had been a source of constant frustration to the Hartzell family, however. Now, as she began to cut the crusts off the bread, she decided to cut the sandwiches into different shapes, rather than the narrow rectangles her mother liked.

"Speaking of new frontiers," Cindy said cautiously as she worked, "there is one thing I should tell you."

"Here it comes."

Cindy pulled the edges off the star sandwich and began working on the next one—a lightning bolt. "Relax, Mom. I think you'll like this."

Her mother stopped working and looked at her.

"I'm moving back to Yazoo City. I'm going to stay this time. As a matter of fact, I've bought a business with the money I saved flying those charter flights in Sydney."

"A business? What kind of business?"

"A flying business," she said. "Two planes, a hangar..."

"A flying business?" her mother asked. "You don't mean..."

"That's right, Mama," she said with a smile. "Your little girl's gonna be a crop duster."

DUSTY PULLED HIS TRUCK into the church parking lot and scanned the faces in the crowd. The picnic had been going on for hours and most of the food had

probably been eaten. Still, he hoped somebody might
have saved him something. He got out of his truck,
grabbed his baseball mitt in case someone cooked up
a game later on, and started toward a cluster of familiar faces.

The first person he saw was Cindy's brother Jake,
surrounded by his four children, and he looked around
until he found Bruce and Paul, Cindy's other brothers. He wondered if they knew yet that she was back
in town, or how she planned to make a living. The
absurdity of the whole thing—his losing his business
to some flaky blonde—almost made him turn around
and go home. But he was going to have to learn to live
with it sooner or later. Might as well start now.

He started toward Jake, with whom he'd gone to
school years ago, and started to ask him if he'd heard
from Cindy, when he heard a flurry behind him.
Turning around, he saw Cindy Hartzell getting out of
her Porsche, still dressed in those obscene shorts and
that shirt that buttoned down over her bikini top and
was tied at the waist. She dressed like Daisy Mae in
"Li'l Abner," he thought, but there was a touch of
class to her that allowed her to pull off such a style
without looking country.

As she pranced by, chin held high and that mischievous smile on her face, people began to whisper and
flutter. A few greeted her, one or two hugged her, but
all the while her mother walked stiffly beside her, as if
she'd been eating a lemon and hadn't got the taste out
of her mouth just yet.

He watched as her father looked up from his fishing pole and saw her, slowly came to his feet, and didn't show a hint of expression on his leathery face. Following suit, her brothers greeted her one by one, each with an initial smile in their eyes that was quickly quelled and replaced with coolness.

What had she done to warrant such a reception? Were all the stories he'd heard about her true? He watched as she set down a basket, around which nephews and nieces flocked, oohing and aahing over the funny shapes of her tuna sandwiches. Slowly, and with great deliberation, Cindy went in turn to each brother, stood on her toes and hugged them. Although they made no attempt to push her away, it was more than obvious that the embraces were all one-sided.

Still, she forged on, and when she reached her father, Dusty thought he saw tears in her eyes. She reached up to hug him, but he backed away. "What are you doing here, Cindy?" he asked brusquely.

Cindy stepped back and gazed up at him. "I missed all of you, Daddy. I've decided to come home."

"To stay?" her father asked.

"Yes," she said. "I have plans, Daddy."

"Do what you want," her father said gruffly. "But whatever it is, don't expect my help. I learned a long time ago to stay out of your problems."

Cindy turned back to her brothers. "I've bought a business," she said. "Webb's Flying Service."

From his place in the shade against the tree, Dusty winced and glanced around, hoping no one else had heard.

Jake's brow wrinkled. "Dusty sold out to you? Really?"

"Yep. I'm keeping him as chief pilot. I'll be crop-dusting, too, though."

"What?" It was Paul's turn, and he glared at her. "Cindy, don't be crazy. You'll kill yourself."

"No, I won't. I'm a terrific pilot. Besides, it's a done deal. I'm here to stay."

Bruce rolled his eyes. "Between relationships, are we?"

Cindy shook her head. "Actually, it has nothing to do with my love life, Bruce."

"Why not? Every other major decision you've ever made has had to do with it."

"That was then," she said. "I've grown up."

"Yeah, right." He peered at her from beneath his heavy lashes, and Dusty could have sworn he saw the hint of a smile in his eyes. But then Bruce glanced toward his father, saw him scowling his way, that indifference returned.

"You look good," said Paul, who was closest in age to Cindy. "Still turning heads everywhere you go."

"It was a long, hot ride," she said. She glanced toward her mother, who was unpacking the baskets, and added, "I haven't even taken my suitcases out of the car yet. Don't know where I'm going to stay tonight."

No answer. Her mother didn't even look up, and her father's scowl only grew more defined. Her brothers, who all lived in their own homes on the Hartzell acreage, didn't make a move. Dusty watched her struggle against defeat as she gave a tiny shrug and grabbed the softball out of Paul's hand. "Anybody up for a game?"

Her brothers were slow to join her, but as Cindy tossed the ball from one hand to another and pranced out to the center of the field, others began to follow.

Dusty held back, and instead of going toward the field, he walked toward her brothers. "Hey, Jake, how are you doing?" he asked, shaking his old friend's hand.

"Hey, Dusty. Heard about the catastrophe you just got yourself caught in."

Dusty peered out toward the field at the woman who had managed to draw nearly every man on the grounds, married or not, into the game. "Yeah, well. There was no helping it."

"Don't worry," he said. "She'll get tired of it in a few weeks and be out of here."

"So what is it with her?" Dusty asked. "I was watching you. There's a lot of water under that bridge."

"You said it," Jake agreed. "She's pulled some pretty good numbers since she left home. Screws up her life royally, bounces back trying to straighten it out, then blows out again. If I had all the money she's wasted, I could buy the county." As he spoke, Jake watched her, and a slow smile inched across his face.

"Damn, she'll drive you crazy. And the worst thing is that she's so hard to be mad at."

"So why fake it?"

Jake shrugged. "It's not faking, really. She exasperates me. And my father has this idea that she needs to be taught a lesson. That we're not going to be her safety net anymore. We agreed to stop bailing her out."

As they spoke, they watched Paul, the youngest brother, chase her from first to second and tag her out. In return, she grabbed him around the neck and began knuckling his head. Laughing, Paul grabbed her wrist and twisted it behind her back.

"Look at him," Jake said on a chuckle. "Dad's gonna kill him. He couldn't give her the cold shoulder if his life depended on it. When she leaves this time, Dad'll come down really hard on Paul. He'll probably blame him that she didn't learn her lesson."

Dusty sighed. "You have any suggestions about how I should handle her?"

Jake laughed. "Just don't let her kill herself," he said, grabbing his glove and pounding a fist into it. "And whatever you do, don't fall in love with her."

IT DIDN'T MATTER who won the game; all that most of the players cared about was horsing around with the woman who'd become something of a legend in Yazoo County. Her laughter echoed over the field, lifting spirits that didn't want to be lifted. Dusty played along, frustrated at the attention she garnered, knowing that by morning everybody in town would know that he'd sold out to her. The thought made him want to go home and sulk, and yet he felt inexorably drawn to her, as if she had some magic pull on him that he couldn't fight.

She flirted shamelessly with every single man around her, then shot looks at Dusty, as if checking to see if he, too, was affected by the sprite who had shaken up the picnic.

But that free spiritedness faltered a bit when it grew dark and the cars began pulling away. One by one, he watched her say goodbye to her brothers, then her parents, not one of them inviting her home with them. Pretending it didn't matter, she busied herself cleaning up, until almost everyone was gone. And as much as Dusty knew he should leave her to her own thoughts, he dismissed his judgment and started toward her.

Cindy heard his voice, deep and rough, before she saw him.

"So did you ever find a place to stay tonight?"

She glanced back at him over her shoulder, noted the glimmer of perspiration on him and the way his wet tank top stuck to his body. His jaw was shaded by end-of-day stubble, and he smelled uniquely male. Even in the darkness, she could see the blue of his eyes . . . a pale blue that softened the tough facade he offered her.

"I'll probably just drive to Jackson and find a hotel."

"There's no need for that," he said.

She dropped the paper plates she'd gathered into a garbage bag and looked up at him. "If you're thinking of inviting me to spend the night with you, no thanks. No matter how wild you've heard I am, I don't fall into bed with virtual strangers."

Dusty grinned. "I wasn't thinking of inviting you to my bed. Actually, the thought hasn't crossed my mind."

She matched his grin and lifted her chin higher. "Oh, no? What, then?"

"I thought you should know that you already own a place where you can stay. There's an apartment upstairs in the hangar. I lived there before I built my house."

Her eyebrows arched instantly. "Really?"

"It's a little dirty," he said. "In fact, it hasn't been cleaned in months. And I'll have to go home and get you some sheets and towels. But there's a shower, and a bed . . ."

She looked up at him, not saying a word, and for a moment, he thought she was going to flex that pride he saw in her eyes, that pride that said she couldn't be knocked down, not even with no place to stay and no one in town genuinely glad to see her. But then she surprised him. A smile broke out over her face and sunlight painted through her eyes as she stood on her toes and threw her arms around him. "See?" she said, looking up at him. "I knew everything was going to fall into place."

For a moment he let her stand like that, her breasts pressed shamelessly against him, and her smile tilted up to him, casting her own warm rays of sunshine on him. He wondered why her boldness made him so uncomfortable, when he usually played the rogue around women and put them on the defensive. But Cindy wasn't like any other woman he knew. "Uh...don't get carried away," he said. "You might really hate it. You're probably used to a lot better."

"Don't bet on it," she said. "I'm sure it's perfect."

He looked down at her, feeling the heat of her body radiating into him, drawing heat from places he'd long forgotten. But as arousing as she was, he knew better than to foster this feeling, or act on her seeming willingness. Having her live in the hangar would be disastrous. It would drive him nuts. But sooner or later she would have found it, anyway, and he couldn't stand the thought of her being left standing here in the dark, all alone, with no place to go.

"I wouldn't do this anymore if I were you," he rumbled, barely touching her hips.

"Do what?" she whispered, knowing full well what he meant.

"Stand here with your arms around me, pressing those beautiful breasts against my chest and thinking that I'll conduct myself like a gentleman."

Her smile was almost wicked. "Oh, Dusty. I know better than to think that."

He wet his lips and took her wrists in his hands, pulled them from around his neck and slid them down his chest. "I thought you had your rules about falling into bed with strangers. Getting involved with people you work with...."

"But I've been breaking rules since I was five years old." Still smiling, she withdrew her hands and stepped back. "Of course, I'm trying to stop. If I don't clean up my act, I'll never earn the right to be a Hartzell again. You're right, Dusty. I won't touch you again."

Grinning like a conqueror asserting authority over her captives, she started to turn away. Something inside him snapped, and Dusty reached out and grabbed her, jerking her against him. Startled, she looked up at him with big eyes that made her look more vulnerable than he'd seen her yet.

She gasped, and Dusty took advantage of her open mouth, slamming his own mouth against it. His tongue rammed against hers, probing without invitation, violating the sweetness with a hungry urgency. Backing her to the tree behind her, he crushed her against it and pressed his body into hers. He reached for the fists she had against his chest and moved them above her head, holding them together there as his other hand gripped her face for his reckless probing of her mouth.

When he broke the kiss, she caught her breath, stunned, and stared up at him.

"Don't play with me, Cindy," he rumbled. "I don't like to be played with."

Suddenly he released her, and she stepped back as he turned and strode to his truck. "I'll meet you at the hangar in fifteen minutes," he said.

Cindy was speechless as she watched him drive away.

THE HANGAR WAS DARK when she arrived at it, and it occurred to her that she hadn't gotten a key from him yet. It didn't really matter, she thought, there was plenty of time for that later.

She got out of her car and slid onto the hood, leaned back against the windshield and looked up at the stars twinkling like an audience above her. "Yeah, I know what you're thinking," she said to them. "You're thinking that I've gotten myself caught in a fire storm with nothing but a paper umbrella. But you're wrong. I can handle Dusty Webb."

The cool March breeze whispered its argument around her, and she shook her head. "He doesn't know what he's dealing with, but he will soon. And so will my family. I'll prove myself to all of them."

She heard a car drive by and quickly sat up to look back. It wasn't Dusty.

Wilting back down, she focused on the stars again. "Dusty Webb," she whispered, letting the name mix with the sound of the breeze. "What a man." A tiny thrill swept through her as she thought of the way he'd grabbed her and kissed her tonight, reaching into the heart of her and pulling out a desire so keen that even she wasn't sure she could deny it. And that was spooky, since she was the Master of Denial. Or the Mistress. Either way, she was the one who looked trouble square in the face and laughed.

She did it with men, too. As much as she liked them, as big a flirt as she was known to be, the plain simple thought of getting close to any of them frightened her even more than shooting like a comet down a barren highway, or flying a plane until the fuel tank ran dry. She supposed that was why she tried so hard to be in control where men were concerned. If she took that attraction by the tail, looked at it head-on, then it was easier to deny it and back away, as if she wasn't that interested. It confused men, frustrated them and more than a few of them had made her their mission in life. She'd run from all of them. All except one, and that had been enough of a mistake to last the rest of her life.

But Dusty wasn't going to let her have the control, she thought with a nervous smile. He had seen her game and had turned it back on her.

Working with him was going to be harder than she thought.

She heard a car and saw Dusty's headlights on the hangar. Sitting up, she turned back to him. He pulled into a parking space, got out and tossed her a set of keys.

"You know," she said, "for someone who hated the idea of my owning this business, you sure are being cooperative."

He shrugged and used his own key to open the front door. A light came on, and he went in and glanced back at her as she followed him. "It's not like I can change things. And I'm not the kind of guy who leaves a girl with no place to sleep."

"Unlike my brothers."

"Your brothers are trying to teach you a lesson. One that you, no doubt, need to learn."

"Then why aren't you going along with them?" she asked.

His smile was foreboding. "You haven't seen this place yet. I have a feeling you can still learn some lessons here."

He went back outside and got a bag out of the bed of his truck. Cindy followed him and grabbed her own suitcase out of her back seat.

She trailed him back into the hangar, walking between the planes to the steps leading up to the door she hadn't noticed before.

The steps creaked beneath his weight, and when he opened the door, she tried to peer in over his shoulder. He reached in and flicked a light switch, but nothing happened.

"Just what I was afraid of," he said. "The bulb's out." He retrieved a flashlight and a bulb from his bag, went into the dark room and changed the bulb on the fixture. As soon as it was screwed in, the light flickered on.

Cindy looked around at the dust covering the floor and the cobwebs in the corners. "How long since you've been up here?"

He reached up and swatted away the webs. "About a year and a half ago. The pilots who worked for me lived here during the season."

He stripped the sheets off the bed, sending a cloud of dust floating through the air. "I hope you don't have any dust allergies."

She reached into his bag and pulled out the sheets he'd brought. "Actually, I'm tougher than I look. I once slept in a swamp with alligators snapping at my toes."

He couldn't help laughing. "Well, up here there are just rodents." He grinned as her face paled noticeably. "That doesn't bother you, does it?"

She lifted her chin and flicked her hair back over her shoulder. "I'll make pets out of them. They'll be housebroken by morning."

She set her suitcase on the bed and went to the dusty mirror on the wall. Raising her arms, she tied her hair in a knot at her crown, then set about tucking the rest of it into a bun that held of its own accord.

He stood motionless while she worked, and finally, when she was almost done, he ambled up behind her. "The bathroom's through that door. I know there's still hot water because I use it downstairs."

His voice was disturbingly close to her ear, and she shivered in spite of her efforts not to.

"I guess you had enough to eat at the picnic."

She hadn't eaten much at all, but she smiled and turned back to him. "I'll be fine."

He stared down at her, and for a moment, a nervous anticipation shot through her. Suddenly, she felt awkward. Shy. And she countered it the way she always had.

"So are you going to wear a tank top again Monday, so I can drool over that sexy chest of yours?"

The edges of his lips curved up slightly.

"What?" she asked innocently.

"Nothing," he said. "I'm just trying to figure you out."

"Well, now, there's an aspiration. Nobody's been able to do it yet. Not even me."

She leaned over and started making up the bed, and after a moment of watching her, Dusty turned and started for the door. "There's a telephone downstairs in the office. My number's in the memory. Call if you need anything."

"Dusty?" she said, before he could get out the door.

He caught his hand on the casing above his head and turned back. "Yeah?"

"Thanks for the room."

He shrugged, further exaggerating the swell of his biceps. "You do own it."

"I know. But you didn't have to help me out tonight."

He dropped his hand and rubbed the grin working at his face again. "Well, I guess you owe me one, then."

"Yeah," she said. "Maybe I'll add a little bonus to your next paycheck."

His grin faded as hers came to life, and he closed the door behind him.

Chapter Four

The March afternoon sun shone down on Dusty's bare chest with July force as he sat on the front porch of his house and watched his dog drag up a dead water moccasin and drop it at his feet. "Nice going, Moon-baby," he said, reaching down to scratch behind the dog's ear.

He heard a car coming up his drive and rose to his feet, wondering who would be coming here on a Sunday. Any visitor would be deliberate since his house was situated so far back from the road that you had to know it was there to find it. He waited until the car came into sight, and seeing that it was Cindy's, he dropped back into his chair.

Her top was up, and it wasn't until she got out that he was able to get a good look at her. If she'd been the stuff of fantasies yesterday, she looked even better to-day, he thought. Her hair was freshly washed and pulled up in a French twist, and she wore a soft sweater and a pair of jeans that did little to hide the shape of the hips they covered. But he buried the at-

traction. That crack about his paycheck last night—
reminding him who was ultimately in control—still
smarted.

Smiling, she started up the porch steps.

"How'd you find me?" he asked, not bothering to
get up.

"Easy. I stopped at Grady's Grocery. He knows
where everybody lives."

"Shoulda known," he said, rolling his eyes. "When
I built the house in such a private place, I knew Grady
wouldn't let it be private for long."

"Do you want me to leave?" she asked him.

He shrugged. "No. I'm just not used to company
dropping in. So how's it going? Did the mice keep you
company last night?"

"Let's just say they did their share of scratching
around. I'm getting a cat today."

"Then you plan to keep living there?"

She shrugged. "I thought I would. It's fine for a
while." She glanced at his house, built like a two-story
log cabin. "This is nice. Did you build it?"

"Yeah, a couple of years ago. I—" He stopped cold
as she caught sight of the dead snake and gasped.
"Don't worry. It's dead. Moon-baby just dragged it
up."

Letting out her breath, Cindy squatted and petted
the dog behind his ears. He moaned in pleasure and
nuzzled his head further against her hand. Dusty sup-
pressed his grin at the impeccable taste of his pet.
"Moon-baby? Where'd you ever get a name like
that?" she asked the dog.

"My niece named him," Dusty said. "She was into Indians at the time and thought it sounded appropriate."

"Well, it does, kind of," she said, scratching her fingernails down the dog's back. "With this pretty black coat, Moon-baby is a great name."

She reached down to touch the dead snake, and instead of recoiling, as he would have expected, she grabbed it by the head and held it up to study it. "Pretty snake," she said. "You should have it mounted."

He grinned at her tenacity. "You like snakes, do you?"

She shrugged. "I dream about them a lot."

His eyes narrowed as he tried harder to figure her out. "Well, you know what that means."

"Yeah, I've heard." She stood up and saw his cat inching around the porch. "A cat, too? What's his name?"

"Dog."

"No." She picked up the cat and brought it to her face. "You're kidding."

"Nope."

"Why would you name your cat Dog?"

"Just to be obnoxious, I guess," he said, coming to his feet. "You want to come in?"

She set the cat down. "Yeah, for a minute. But the real reason I came by was to get the keys to the planes. I wanted to take one up this afternoon, kind of check out the land, but I couldn't find them anywhere."

His smile collapsed, and he opened the door. "Don't you think you could wait until tomorrow? I mean, I'll be there, and—"

"No, Dusty. I'd really like to do it now."

With a martyred sigh, he led her into the house. She looked around at the rustic living room, the loft overhead and the wing leading to the bedrooms. "Nice," she said. "It looks so well kept."

"Well kept? What do you mean?"

"Well, most bachelors have garage-sale furniture and laundry thrown over the chairs."

"Yeah, well. I like where I live to be comfortable."

"It's a lot of space for one person," she said, taking the liberty to stroll to the bedroom door and peer in. His bed was huge, and its dark green comforter matched the drapes. White carpet padded the floor, and the room had that scent she already associated with him—unidentifiable after-shave and maleness. "Have you always lived here alone?"

"Who else would have lived here?" His lazy Southern drawl was tinged with indifference and just a hint of contempt.

"Well, I don't know. A wife. A girlfriend."

"I built this for myself," he said. "I've never been married, and I haven't found anyone I'd be interested in sharing it with." He walked up behind her and looked at her as she freely inspected his bedroom.

She looked over at him, swept her eyes down his chest, then slowly smiled. "What a waste," she said.

He grinned. "The house or the man?"

"Both," she said. Then, before he could react, she slipped past him and started back to the living room. "So where's the key?"

His mood took a nosedive again, and he led her into the kitchen, a huge room with an island in the middle. He reached up and took a set of keys off a hook on the cabinet and handed it to her. "I don't like letting people fly my planes," he said.

She looked up at him. "They're my planes now," she said. "I'll have another set of the keys made today, though, so you can have one for the plane you'll be flying."

"And which one would that be?" he asked, his tone taking on a sharp edge.

"The turbine, I think," she said, indicating the better of the two planes. "You'll be doing most of the work until I get to know the farms and get better at flying. I'll take the Ag Cat until then."

"You sure you want to do this?" he asked. "Fly, I mean? You could just leave that to me, and concentrate on marketing and bookkeeping and stuff yourself."

"I'm not a bookkeeper, I'm a pilot," she said. "And after I do a little marketing, we'll have so much business that we'll need a second pilot. No need to hire somebody else when I can do it myself. Besides, I can't wait. It's going to be great."

"It could be a slow season," he said. "It may not even be necessary."

She smiled. "Don't kid yourself. We had such a mild winter that the bugs didn't have time to die out.

They should be in great form this year. I've been praying for boll weevils all winter." Tossing the keys into the air and catching them with one hand, she started back to the door.

"Wait. I'll go with you."

"That's not necessary," she said.

"Yes, it is. You should never fly when no one's manning the hangar. For one thing, it's not good to leave it open, where anyone can come in. And for another, if something happens to you, no one will know you're down."

"You were alone when I drove up yesterday."

He faltered. "Well . . . that's different."

"How?"

"Well, I shouldn't have been, okay? I just haven't been able to hire anybody this year."

Her smile was half-cocked. "Don't worry about me. I'm a good pilot. The engines don't have many hours on them, and when I checked them out this morning they looked very well maintained."

"They are very well maintained." He sighed and followed her out the door. "Look, Cindy, all sorts of things can happen. There are power lines across some of these fields that are hard to see. And no matter how well maintained an engine is, there are times when they fail. I've crash-landed myself, twice. It's not fun."

"I don't imagine it is," she said. "That last time almost did you in." She glanced over him and drew her brows together. "What happened to you, anyway? Your lawyer said you'd been in the hospital for months and that you couldn't fly at all last season. But you don't exactly look handicapped."

He smiled at the offhanded compliment. "I broke both legs and my back. I've worked hard to put myself back together."

"And what a job you've done," she said, that maddening grin intruding again. "You're right, I've never crashed, but it might make you feel better to know I've made three emergency landings. One for faulty landing gear, one because a poacher shot a hole in my fuel tank and it caught fire, and one because lightning struck my wing."

He frowned, and she could see that he didn't entirely believe her. "How long have you been flying?"

"About five years," she said. "Long enough to build a nest egg and buy a business. Flying is a natural occupation for me. I've always been so good at flying by the seat of my pants."

Despite himself, he grinned. "Are you still doing that?"

"I'll always be doing that," she said. "A girl doesn't go into crop-dusting because she likes nine-to-five work."

As if he'd heard enough, he grabbed his wallet off a table, stuffed it into his back pocket and started for the door. "I'm coming to the hangar with you."

She shrugged. "Do what you want, but I *don't* need a baby-sitter."

"No, but you may need someone to dig you out of the plane before the day's over, after you've had a run-in with that adrenaline of yours. Do you even have a helmet?''

She laughed. "A helmet? What good is that gonna do?''

"If you crash, they'll find your brains all in one place. You have to wear one."

She gave him a skeptical look over her shoulder. "Oh, do I really?''

"Yes," he said, not backing down. "The helmet saved my life last time. I have an extra one in the office, but you'll need to have one of your own made. It'll fit better."

"Wait a minute," she said. "I have *never* flown with a helmet."

"Well, you're going to start now if you want me to train you. The first thing is to put a helmet on. And there are a few other things you need to know about the plane before you take off."

She rolled her eyes. "Look, I didn't come over here to drag you back to work on Sunday. I really can do this myself. I've flown all types of planes, crop-dusters included, and I know what I'm doing."

"You don't know the personality of *my* planes," he said. "If you're smart, you'll take advantage of my willingness to work with you."

She sighed. "All right, hotshot. I'll meet you at the hangar."

"Promise me that you won't do anything stupid until I get there."

She smirked. "Oh, now, I can't make a promise like that." She got into her car, grinning. "Hurry. I'm itching to get going."

Dusty cursed under his breath as she skidded out of sight.

CINDY HAD NO SOONER pulled up to the hangar than her oldest and youngest brothers, Jake and Paul, pulled in behind her. Smiling, Cindy bounced out.

"Hey, guys."

They got out of the truck, and the agitated look on their faces was unmistakable. Ignoring their expressions, Cindy pressed a kiss on each of their cheeks.

"Where have you been?" Jake asked her.

"Here—where else?"

"We looked for you all night," Paul said. "I must have called every hotel from Yazoo City to Jackson. What did you do? Go home with Dusty?"

"No. There's an apartment upstairs. Why were you looking for me?"

"Because we wanted to make sure you had a place to stay," Paul said.

Cindy laughed, unlocked the front door to the hangar and led them in. "Well, you sure didn't act like you cared last night. I hinted every way I knew, and I didn't even get a nibble."

Jake sighed. "We couldn't say anything in front of Dad."

"Oh, right," she said. "If you did anything as rebellious as giving your sister a place to sleep, there's no telling what he might do."

"Look, Cindy." Paul, who had always been closest to her, plopped down on the desk. "You've got to understand where we're coming from. We work for Dad. We've got a good thing going. If we make him mad—"

"If you make him mad, he might disown you like he's done me." She laughed and shook her head. "Wake up, guys. It's not the worst thing in the world. I'm still here, aren't I?"

"Don't act like you don't care," Jake said. "You wouldn't be back here if you didn't."

Cindy sank down onto the sofa against the wall. "All right. I do care. But not because of what Mom and Dad can do for me."

"Why, then?"

"Because I miss my family," she said seriously. "I've been everywhere, done everything, had everything, seen everything…and what I've learned is that everybody needs a home. Even me. And I don't give one whit whether I ever get back in their wills."

"But we care," Jake said. "I've invested years of my life in Dad's enterprises, but it's all still his. He could cut me off just like that. I can't risk that."

Cindy got to her feet again and went to her oldest brother, who stood looking at her with deep worry etched into his face. He looked so much older than he had when she'd last seen him. "Jake, Dad isn't a monster. He doesn't cut his children off on a whim. Think of all the things I've done. It took a lot for him to turn on me."

"It gets easier with practice," he said, "and Dad hasn't been the same since you've been out of the family. He's more rigid than ever, harder to reason with, and he doesn't leave a lot of room for sentiment or emotion. Not that he ever did."

"Then I'll come back into the family," she said, as if that solved everything. "Whether he likes it or not." She smiled and put her arms around Jake's neck. "Don't worry. I'm not going to run out this time. I'm here to stay. I love Yazoo City, and I've missed it. And I'm excited about my new business—"

She heard Dusty's car pulling up outside, and then his car door closing. In seconds, the door opened, and Dusty strode in. "Hey, Jake . . . Paul."

As they greeted each other, she noted that he'd put on a shirt . . . not the usual tank top, but a blue chambray shirt with one too many buttons buttoned and not enough chest showing through. She made a note to mention it to him later.

"Anyway . . ." Jake turned back to her, as if finishing a sentence. "We came by to tell you that if you want to stay at either mine or Paul's house, you're welcome, as long as you keep a low profile."

Cindy's smile was sad. "Thanks, guys. But I'll just stay here."

Paul wrinkled his nose and looked around. "No offense to Dusty, but it's not quite like a home."

Dusty shrugged. "None taken. And you're right. It's not like your typical Hartzell digs, but there aren't many places in town that are."

Cindy shook her head. "I'm staying, guys. I like it here. It's mine." She reached for the helmet perched on a shelf behind the desk and pulled it on. "So you don't have to worry about stepping on Dad's toes. And Bruce can go on being righteously indignant at his renegade sister. Nobody has to change their way of thinking. And nobody has to lose anything because of me."

She pulled the keys Dusty had given her out of her pocket and started into the hangar part of the building. "I'm ready to get started, Dusty. I'll do a preflight."

Dusty watched her walk away and didn't miss the fragile way she held her mouth, as if she might crumble and cry with one more exchange. Somehow, he felt a twist of sympathy for her, an illogical protectiveness against her brothers.

"Are you really gonna let her fly that thing?" Paul asked Dusty when she was gone.

Dusty breathed a helpless laugh. "Hey, she owns everything here."

"That's just like her," Jake said. "Going off halfcocked and buying a business without a thought." Jake peered through the door to where she was busy inspecting the wings for anything that could cause problems in flight. "Look, Dusty," he said in a conspiratorial voice. "She's not the most rational person in the world."

"Nor the most responsible," Paul interjected.

"You need to watch her. Don't let her mess up and kill herself."

Dusty laughed. "I'm doing my best. Why do you think I'm here now?"

He looked toward her again and saw that she was balanced on a ladder, examining the engine. He could see that she knew what she was doing by the way she put her hands inside and worked.

"I wonder if she needs any money." Paul reached into his back pocket for his wallet, and Dusty stopped him.

"She just bought my business. She drives a Porsche. Somehow I don't think she's hurting."

"Oh, yeah." He slid it back into his pocket. "I wonder how she got all that money. She didn't get any from her divorce, did she?"

Jake shrugged. "Maybe she got it from that count guy she was seeing. He was loaded."

"Or maybe the British royal family paid her off to stay away." Paul shot his brother a look. "What do you think?"

Jake shook his head. "Nah. Too farfetched."

"Well, wherever she got it, she got it...it's hers."

Dusty said goodbye and watched Cindy's two brothers amble back to their truck. Then he turned back to her.

She was perched on the ladder, examining the engine in the nose of the plane. "There's fluid splattering from somewhere, Dusty. Looks like it could be this hose here. Have you had it checked out?"

Dusty gave her a surprised look. "Yeah. As a matter of fact, I had the mechanic here last week. He replaced that hose, but I haven't had the chance to clean it up yet."

"Good," she said. "It seemed strange since I couldn't find a leak anywhere."

She wiped her hands on a rag, then made her way down. "Did my brothers leave?"

"Yeah, they're gone."

She smiled. "They're worried about me. Sweet, huh?"

"If you don't mind them doing it in the closet."

"Yeah, well, you have to know my father. He makes things hard."

She grabbed her helmet off the floor and pulled herself up onto a wing.

"But you're his daughter. Doesn't he wish you well?"

"Of course he does. He just can't make himself show it right now. He loves me."

"Maybe, as long as it's easy."

Opening the plane's door, she stepped into the cockpit. When she was seated, she looked down at him. "For a man who's always alone except for a dog named Moon-baby and a cat named Dog, you sure have some strong opinions about relationships."

"Who says I'm always alone?"

"I watched you at the picnic yesterday. You have your share of women who perk up at the sight of you, but that's strictly physical. What do you really know about the intimate side of love? What does any man know?"

"More than you, I'll bet," he said, angrily hoisting himself up onto the wing. He got to the open door and bent in to face her. "I've never run from one country to another looking for a higher rush than the one I had before. And I've never collected women like trophies, the richer and better-known the better, and I've never married on a whim and then divorced on a bigger one."

Her face reddened as she glared at him. "Oh, I do love the way the Yazoo City grapevine keeps informed of my exploits." She set some of the controls, then stopped and stared at the instrument panel. "It's easy for you, isn't it? Everything's always been worked out, nice and easy. You're dug in here, where you grew up, and you never have to leave this nice safe little nest. Well, it's not that easy for some people, Dusty. Some of us take risks, and sometimes we fail. Excuse me. I'm going to pull the plane out of the hangar now. Do you like to taxi it out, or pull it out with the truck?"

"It should be pulled out or the engine will blow trash and stuff into the hangar, but I—"

She pulled out of her seat and climbed back out, almost knocking him off the wing. "Fine. I'll have to use your truck. I don't have a bumper hitch."

"Wait a minute." He jumped down after her and stopped her before she could get out the door. "I know about failure. Why the hell do you think I'm standing here talking to you?"

"You had some bad breaks. Excuse me if I'm not drowning in pity, but you got off pretty easy if you ask me. You could do a lot worse than having me for a boss."

She jerked away from his arm, opened the sliding doors to the hangar, then latched the tow bar to the wheels of the plane.

"And by the way," she said, flinging around before she went to his truck. "I like you better in a tank top. Who do you think you're trying to kid with that shirt buttoned up to your throat, anyway?"

As if the thought made her indignant, she got into the truck, cranked it and backed it around toward the plane.

"Yeah, well, I feel the same way about that shirt you're wearing. It doesn't hide anything, you know."

She got out of the truck and slammed the door. "You told me to cover up, so I covered up!"

He bent over and hooked the tow bar over the truck's bumper hitch. Under his breath, he mumbled, "You could wear a potato sack and still..."

His words trailed off, and Cindy stepped back onto the wing. "Tomorrow I will."

"Tomorrow you will what?"

"Wear a potato sack," she said. "Now, if you'll pull the plane out, I'll be on my way."

Dusty slammed into the truck and pulled the plane out, got it into position for takeoff, then unhitched the truck and got it out of the way. By the time he got back to her, she had cranked the plane's engine and was studying the controls carefully.

He leaned back against his holding tank and crossed his arms, brooding at their exchange while she pulled her helmet on, plugged the radio into the earpiece, waved to him and started down the strip.

It wasn't until she had lifted off and took a tight turn to the right, that he realized he was about to be in for the flight of his life.

Chapter Five

"Come in, Dusty. I know you can hear me. I turned the radio on this morning."

Dusty tore his eyes from the plane circling overhead and, rather than going into the office to answer, reached into his truck for his radio mike. "Come in, Cindy. Don't you know FCC regulations? You can't just call me up like that. You have to use a call number. Over."

"Well, I don't have one, do I?"

He groaned. "You use the number for our base unit. It's written at the top of the radio. Over."

"Affirmative," she said in a pseudoserious tone. "Let's start over. I'll say, 'MTX952B, this is MTX952B, come in.' But with the same number, how will I know if I'm you or me?"

"You're Mobile 2. Mobile 1 is in my truck! Oh, just forget it!" he shouted. "What do you want?"

He heard her laughter over the radio. "Can you see where I am?"

He squinted into the sunlight. "Yeah, I see you. Over."

"Whose farm am I coming up on? The big L-shaped one."

"That'd be the Wilsons' place. I just defoliated it last week. They're planting cotton in that big stretch, and beans in the other part."

"You forgot to say 'over,'" she said. "Now, how are we ever going to communicate if you insist on breaking the rules?"

Grinding his jaw together, he refused to humor her with an answer.

Again, she laughed. "Do you think they'd mind if I practice over that field?"

He stiffened and looked up at her. "What do you mean? Practice what?"

"Crop-dusting," she said. "I need to practice diving and climbing in this plane. Will they mind or not?"

He hesitated for a long moment, then realized there wasn't anything in the hopper for her to spray. "You won't get a true feel for it without anything in the hopper. Even water would give you a better idea of the weight of the plane. Over."

"I know that," she snapped back. "I can still practice."

He clicked his mike. "All right. I'm sure it's okay, as long as you don't crash and start the field on fire. Over."

"Real funny," she said.

"Before you do, get a good look at that electrical wire that cuts through it. And those trees on the other side are higher than they look. Over."

"Roger, wilco," she said. "Over and out."

He rolled his eyes at her facetiousness and set the mike back on its handle, then walked out to watch her as she made a descent. She was going down too fast, he thought, and as she disappeared behind the trees, he got a sick feeling in his gut. What if she underestimated the weight of the plane or the power in the controls? What if she took it too low?

He held his breath and waited, listening for the sound of her plane humming in the distance. But she was too far away. Squinting, he stared in her direction, waiting for her to ascend and miss the trees, but she didn't come up. "Damn," he said.

Quickly, he jumped into his truck and tried to call her again. "Come in, Cindy. Where the hell are you?"

No answer. Panicked, he cranked his truck and started to drive out after her, but realized that the Wilson farm wasn't easy to get to. It would be quicker to fly over and find her.

"Damn woman," he said as he backed his truck around, got out and hitched the plane to the tow bar to pull it out, then got in and cranked it. Once inside the plane he snapped his helmet on and plugged in his radio. As he started his takeoff, he tried calling her again. "Come in, Cindy. Come in."

Still no answer. He tried to breathe as he lifted off and circled around over the trees in the direction of the Wilson farm. In the L-shaped field she had asked him about, there was no sign of her. He scanned the horizon, looking for smoke, but saw nothing.

Suddenly, a voice spoke in his ear. "Come in, Dusty."

"Cindy, where the hell are you?" he shouted.

"Three o'clock," she said, and he glanced to his right and saw her coming up out of another field. "Sorry about the radio. It came unplugged from my helmet. And I had just told you my darkest, most torrid secret. I'll never get the nerve to tell you again."

He didn't know if it was relief or genuine amusement that made him smile, but shaking his head, he said, "You didn't come up. I thought—"

"That I had crashed? Gosh, I sure would have kept the radio on for that. You'd have heard a giant 'ouch.' Actually, I went under the wire, just to see if I could. Good thing there's no cotton yet, or I'd have some on my wheels. Then I squeezed between those two trees on the other side and just kept on going into that other field."

His smile collapsed. "You did what? Are you crazy?"

"You forgot to say 'over,'" she said again. "Over."

"You damn fool, don't *ever* go under a wire. I don't even do that and I've been doing this for over fifteen years!"

"Hey, I cleared it, didn't I?"

"Yeah, this time. And those two trees are too close together. You could have knocked off a wing." Fuming, he barked out, "Over!"

"Or maybe I'm a better pilot than you think," she returned.

"I don't think so, Cindy. Just a more reckless one." He began a turn, heading back toward the hangar, and said, "I'm landing now. If you know what's good for you, you'll do it, too."

"I'm not ready to land," she said. "I'm having fun."

"Damn it, put the plane down! We have to talk."

"Dusty, you keep forgetting to say 'over.' How can we communicate if you don't do it right?"

"Put the plane down, Cindy!"

"That's a negative, Dusty. I want to buzz that field to my left first. But you go ahead."

He tried to remember how much fuel was in her plane. Maybe she'd run low before she killed herself. Looking back out his window, he watched as she took a dive, skirting as low as he did over the land, then pulled into a quick climb just before hitting the trees. Circling around, he saw the skill with which she turned herself around and took another dive across the field. It riled him that she was as good as she was. If there was anything he hated, it was a hotshot rookie who had the talent to back up her recklessness.

"This is great," came Cindy's voice in his ear. "I'm gonna love this."

Too angry to answer, he took his own dive, just to show her how a pro did it, and skirted mere feet from the ground, then pulled up just short of the trees and turned almost upside down before angling around and diving again.

"If I admit I'm impressed," she said as she circled around above him, "will you stop being mad at me?"

He refused to answer and pulled up from his descent, making a perfect circle in the sky, turning upside down, then coming under and righting himself.

He heard her laughter over the radio, and a loud whoop. "That was terrific. You should be in the circus. Of course, *I* could do that if I were in the turbine. This engine just doesn't have enough pull."

"You ever try that, Cindy, I'll drown you in the chemical tank myself."

"Oh, right. That trick's only for daredevils like you. I forgot about your monopoly on excitement."

"These planes aren't for excitement, Cindy. They're for making a living."

"Right. Just a job, right? You could just as well be pumping gas."

"Put the plane down, Cindy," he said. "Surely your fuel is running low by now."

"I'll beat you down," she said.

He rolled his eyes at the stupid challenge, but when she put an extra thrust into her plane and turned back to the hangar, he couldn't help turning, too.

She wouldn't dare try to compete with him in landing, he thought. If they got on the runway at the same time, they'd destroy both planes. She was bluffing, and he was going to call it.

He saw her wave one wing at him, then start a descent that was too far into the runway. It was too close for her to stop sufficiently before she reached the hangar, he thought. He hung back, watching with breath held as she dived toward the runway.

Then suddenly, she pulled up, and her laughter played over the radio again. "Scared you, didn't I?"

"You should be in an institution," he returned. "At least one of us will be before this season's over."

"But it won't be boring," she said.

With his radio off and his voice low, he chuckled. "No, it won't be boring."

He made like he was going to land and watched her come in behind him as if to follow him onto the landing strip. Calling her bluff, he went ahead and touched down, and again she pulled up and circled around.

He laughed, not certain whether it was from relief or nervous tension, and when he had brought his plane to a halt and turned it around, he allowed himself to take a deep breath and watch her come in for her landing.

No, it certainly wouldn't be boring, he thought. In spite of his bad luck and his need to sell out, he had the feeling this would be the most interesting season he'd have yet.

Cindy saw him climbing out of his plane when she pulled hers in beside him. As she turned it around, he set his hands on his hips and she could see that old lecture coming on. Just like the ones her brothers used to give her. Just like the ones she got from her father.

But Dusty looked better than all four of them, and she had to admit that she liked riling him. It made for interesting conversation.

She got out of the cockpit, hopped down from the wing, and flashed him a thumbs-up sign. "That was great."

"You almost got yourself killed," he said.

She grinned and pranced toward him. "That why you were matching me stunt for stunt?"

"Hey, I'm a professional. I've been doing this for a decade and a half."

"But you can't back down from a challenge, even from an amateur, can you? I'll have to remember that." He didn't like that, she could see, and chuckling under her breath, she pulled her helmet off.

"Really, Cindy, you can't go around flying under electrical wires. Or telephone wires. Or between trees."

She went to the holding tank and checked its contents. "I think I'm going to fill the hopper with water and do a little spraying. I want to get a feel for a loaded plane."

He shook his head. "You aren't listening to me!"

"I'm listening, I'm listening," she said. "But so far I haven't heard you say anything interesting." She swung around, her eyes brightening. "Tell me about that loop you did, Dusty. How fast did you get at the top of the loop?"

"I don't know. Eighty, I think. Look, if you ever try that..."

"What were your power settings? Did you notice as you were falling out of the circle?"

"Cindy, I mean it. It's easy to die out there. I have friends who've been killed. My father died that way, for God's sake! If you want me to train you, you have to listen."

It was only then that she abandoned the hose she was unreeling and turned her full attention on him. "I am listening, Dusty. Believe it or not, I'm not stupid. I swear. I like life too much to jeopardize it that way. I'm sure you have a lot to teach me, and I plan to absorb every bit of it."

He didn't quite know what to say to that, so he turned on the hose and handed her the tip. "All right, then. It probably is a good idea to fill the hopper. Takeoff's a whole lot different with a full load, and so are the dives. But don't take a long time. The wind's eight miles per hour, and by the end of the day it's supposed to be twelve or so. We don't fly when it's over ten, is that clear?"

"Oh, come on, Dusty," she said. "Do you really abide by that?"

"Damn right, I do," he said. "You respect your plane and the weather around you, Cindy, and you can live a long life as a crop duster. Break the rules, and you're liable to wind up another statistic. The average life span of a crop duster is—"

"I know. Six years," she said, not concerned.

"No," he returned, as if offended. "I thought it was twelve."

"Whatever. It's not like you go up in a puff of smoke when you hit that deadline."

"No, but if you hit that electrical wire you could." He cut off the water, closed the loading valve and started back into the hangar. "She's all yours," he said. "Don't abuse her."

Smiling, Cindy climbed back into the plane.

THE TELEPHONE RANG just as Cindy lifted off, and Dusty went back into the office and answered it, hoping it wasn't a farmer wanting him to work today.

"Dusty Webb."

"Dusty? This is Hyram Hartzell."

Dusty frowned, wondering if he was calling to make amends with Cindy. "Yes, Mr. Hartzell. How are you?"

"Fair," the man said. "But I'm calling about Cindy."

No kidding, Dusty wanted to say. "What about her?" he asked.

"I understand you've sold your business to her. I wondered if that sale was final yet."

"Well, yes, it is. Why?"

The man hesitated. "Well, I thought I might make you a better offer."

Dusty's frown grew more defined. "Why would you want to do that?"

"To keep the girl from killing herself," he said. "She's not rational, you know. She doesn't make sane decisions, and this crop-dusting thing... Well, it's outrageous."

"Actually, it's a pretty good business," Dusty said, not knowing why he felt the need to defend her. "She'll do well."

"I'm not talking about money," her father said. "I'm talking about her breaking her neck."

"I've been watching Cindy fly this afternoon, Mr. Hartzell. She's actually an excellent pilot."

"She totaled her first car when she was fifteen," he said. "The second one a year later. You total a plane, and you don't walk out of it."

"Oh, I don't know," he said, sitting back in his chair, baffled that he felt so argumentative on her behalf. "Sometimes you do."

"Well, you were lucky," Hartzell said. "Are you sure you've closed the deal? She already owns it?"

"I'm afraid so," Dusty assured him. "What would you have done? Bought it out from under her, just to keep her from getting it?"

"Yes, that's exactly what I would have done."

"Well, it looks to me like you could have used that money in a more positive way. In fact, it wouldn't cost a dime to have given her a place to sleep last night."

"My daughter is resourceful," Hartzell said. "I'm sure she had a place to sleep." He paused a moment. "Are you sleeping with her?"

Dusty sat up rigid in his chair. "Excuse me?"

"You heard me."

"I just met her yesterday," Dusty said. "Even I don't work that fast."

"Then why are you defending her?"

"I'm not defending her," Dusty said. "I just think you underestimate your daughter. I can understand a father's concern for his daughter's welfare, but I don't understand this antagonism you have toward her. In my family, no matter what might happen in our lives, or how we screw up, we can always come home."

"You don't know the first thing about my family," Hartzell said. "Or what she's put us through."

Dusty leaned back in his chair and propped his feet on his desk. "Well, forgive me if I don't sympathize a lot. There are families who've endured worse. Like the death of a family member. Once they're gone, you know, they don't ever come back. Cindy could still come back, if you let her."

Hartzell was quiet for a moment. "I had forgotten about your sister, Dusty, and your father was a friend of mine. I understand your point. But it isn't the same thing. Besides, my reason for calling you was to try to keep her *from* killing herself."

"I think you have a problem, Mr. Hartzell," Dusty said. "And maybe you need to try to figure out whether this is about your anger at her or a real fear for her safety."

"Thank you for the amateur psychology. Don't get above yourself, Dusty. You're just a crop duster."

Dusty stiffened again. "Well, maybe now we're getting to the heart of things. Crop-dusting isn't good enough for your daughter, is it? You're ashamed of it."

"She could do better. She's educated, and smart—"

"And so am I," Dusty said, feeling his face turning red. "Contrary to popular belief, Mr. Hartzell, flying a plane isn't a common pastime for morons. It's hard, and it takes immense concentration and mental capacity. I haven't seen Cindy lacking in either of those areas."

"I see," the man said. "So she's got you hood-winked. That's not surprising."

The phone clicked in his ear, and Dusty sat staring at it for a moment. Then, slamming it down, he got up from his chair. Walking outside, he watched Cindy coming up from the Wilson farm, turning, then descending again.

How had she gotten so free spirited, when her parents were so rigid? But wasn't that always the way it went? People never seemed to come from the homes you'd expect of them. Those who hadn't known Dusty all his life would never have suspected the pain and suffering his own family had endured when his little sister, Lilly, had been struck with liver cancer at the age of fifteen. But experiencing death at such close range had made him appreciate those he loved ever since. Life was precious, and health even more so. And there was so little time for playing games and fighting losing battles. If there were points to be made, they were best made blatantly, without all the psychology and lesson-teaching attached. That was how his family had done things since Lilly died.

But the Hartzells weren't like his family, and Cindy wasn't like anyone he'd ever known before. He watched her swoop up as if to make a dangerous loop, and he caught his breath. Then, as if she knew he was watching, she pulled out of the loop and descended again.

She was a game-player, he thought, unlike him. But her games were not for lesson teaching, like her parents' were. Hers were for hiding. That was obvious from the way she flaunted herself at him, then pulled back just when he took the bait. She wasn't what he'd call a tease, exactly. She wasn't the tart type. The desire was all there—he could see it in the way she walked and moved and the way she wore her clothes. Sensuality radiated from her like a potent force she had the power to abuse. Yet he could see it in her eyes, sometimes...that fear of her own sexuality, that fear of what she saw in him.

But she could stand up to him, take the reins of his business and call out her orders with a honey-toned voice. It was the first time he'd met a woman who was a match for him. And it was the first time he'd wanted one this much.

But that was stupid, he told himself. Getting involved with her on any level would be foolish. It was bad enough that she would be his boss. That was tough enough to swallow. But if she had control over his libido, as well, it could be a long, hot summer. Somehow, he had to fight that desire.

But he suspected she wasn't going to help at all.

He watched her circle overhead and come in to land, and he went back inside, so she wouldn't know he'd been watching her. He heard the plane's deep rumble as it slowed beside the hangar, and after a moment the engine cut off.

She was at the office door in moments, her eyes brilliant with excitement and her hair tousled from the helmet she'd just slid off her head. "That's better than sex," she said. "Don't you think?"

He tried not to grin. "Depends on who you've been doing it with," he said in an indolent drawl. "Personally, I don't think it comes close. But that's just me."

Her grin was cocky, and bypassing the chair across from the desk, she slid up onto the desk top itself. "So you're saying that sex with you is more exciting than a power dive from a thousand to six feet in ten seconds?"

He leaned back in his chair, propped his feet on the edge of the desk and crossed his arms behind his head. "You sound pretty curious. Wanna find out?"

She gave him a look that only men were supposed to give, and he felt an uncomfortable stirring in his groin. "Can you take me to places I've never been before?" she asked seductively.

He grinned. "I've been known to."

"I don't know," she said. "I've been just about everywhere."

"Not where I could take you," he said.

For a moment they stared at each other, and he wondered if simply willing her to take her clothes off, one piece at a time, would actually make her do it. She was unpredictable, with that sparkle of amusement in her eyes. She wasn't afraid of him, and yet she was.

Dropping his feet, he stood up and braced his hands on the desk, leaning millimeters from her face. She didn't back away, but he could see the amusement fading from her eyes. If he reached out to touch her, would she cower back, or melt like hot wax in his hands?

"If I were the kind of woman who acted on impulse," she whispered, meeting his eyes, "I might throw you down right here and have my way with you."

He started to laugh, but couldn't decide whether to take her surprising words as prank or premonition. He had no doubt that she could have complete control over him in a matter of minutes. He also had no doubt that he would love every minute of it.

"Go ahead," he said in his best Clint Eastwood voice. "Make my day."

She laughed softly under her breath and ran a fingertip down his throat, to the opening in his shirt where a triangle of hair curled out. "Better not," she said. "If it wasn't as exciting as flying, the disappointment might be unbearable. And my disappointment might devastate your ego so completely that you might never be able to enjoy sex again."

"No," he said, grinning. "That won't happen."

"Just in case," she said, sliding away from him and off the desk, "maybe we'd better just keep each other up here." She tapped her temple. "In our heads."

"In our fantasies?" he asked. "What makes you think I've been fantasizing about you?"

"I'm talking about *my* fantasies," she said with a half grin as she started for the door.

He breathed a frustrated laugh as she disappeared. Dropping back into his chair—her chair now—he shook his head. The woman was going to have control over him in more ways than just business, he thought. No matter how he told himself that he would keep his distance from her, both physically and emotionally, he suspected that she was calling all the shots in this. The moment she gave him the word—or the look or wink or smile—whether she meant it or not, all his decisions about his conduct in this relationship would fly out the window and he would be at her mercy.

He looked out the window and wondered if she knew that. Did she realize the power she had over men? Did she know how big a part she played in his mind when she wasn't around? Did it excite her, or frighten her to death?

He watched her back up the truck, bend over and hook the trailer hitch on. She was busy, he thought, and from the look on her face, she wasn't even thinking about him.

He put up the file he'd been looking at, or pretending to, and ambled outside as she was pulling the plane back into the hangar. When she got out of the truck, she tossed him a matter-of-fact look. "Feel like a burger?"

He shook his head. "Not particularly. Haven't you been to the grocery store yet?"

"Nope. I've been busy."

"So what did you eat for lunch?"

"A burger."

"And you want one again?"

She laughed. "This is Yazoo City. It's not like there's a different cuisine on every corner. Chicken, burgers and pizza...that's about it. And I don't feel like chicken.''

He knew before he opened his mouth that he shouldn't. ''Why don't you let me cook you supper?''

She looked up, slinging her hair back from her face. ''You? Can you cook?''

He frowned. ''Well, yeah. What do you think I eat?''

''I don't know. Chicken, pizza, burgers or whatever your latest girlfriend cooks up for you.''

''I happen to be a very good cook,'' he said. ''And I just happen to have a couple of steaks marinating.''

''A couple? Were you planning to cook for me all day?''

He shook his head at her blatant audacity. ''No, actually, I was saving one to cook for tomorrow. Do you want to come or not?''

She shrugged. ''Well...yeah, okay. That'd be nice.'' She turned away as she said it, and he watched her as she took the trailer hitch off the plane and put it back in its place. ''But how do I know I can trust you? Alone in your house, out in the woods, at night...''

He grinned. ''I think it's yourself you're most afraid of.''

She didn't answer his smile. Instead, he saw a soft sadness pass over her face, but it quickly disappeared. ''No, I'm pretty harmless,'' she said.

He wondered if any man who'd ever been around her for more than ten seconds had found her harmless. ''And so am I.''

She snickered then, and that grin returned. "Yeah, right." She looked up at him, and he saw that spritely humor again. "It doesn't pay to get physically involved with your boss, you know. I could use it against you."

"Tell me about it." He took the keys from her and set about closing the hangar doors. "Truth is, I've already come to that conclusion, Cindy. I'm not crazy about this relationship. I haven't had a boss in over fifteen years, and I don't particularly like starting now. But as long as I have to live with it, we might as well get along. Consider this a goodwill dinner, instead of a seduction. If I were going to seduce you, I wouldn't go to all the trouble of cooking for you."

"Oh, no?" she asked. "What would you do?"

He grinned. "I'd get right down to business. Ten minutes, and you'd be shivering and begging for more. It wouldn't be pretty."

"Ten minutes, huh? And then it would probably be over in twelve, and I'd be shivering out of frustration and disappointment."

Astounded, he turned her to face him, his face startlingly close to hers. "Lady, I don't know who you've been with, but if that's how it was, you've been missing a hell of a lot. With me, it'll take two, three hours. At least. They'll have to call the paramedics and rope off the block."

Her eyes grew smoky. "You're pretty sure of yourself, aren't you?"

"Try me."

She smiled and flipped away. "Not tonight. But I will take you up on the steaks."

Grabbing her arm, he flung her back around, facing her with eyes as amused as her own. "Good, because I wasn't offering anything but steaks tonight."

For a moment their eyes locked, and he saw her rising to the challenge. It was going to be frustrating, it was going to be maddening, it was going to be stimulating. But this dinner tonight—and indeed their whole relationship—was always going to be fun.

Chapter Six

Cindy could see Dusty in the kitchen when she pulled into the driveway, and when he saw her, he opened the door. The music of the BoDeans spilled out, and she went in. "I thought crop dusters only listened to country music."

"Not this one," he said.

She looked over, noted that he was wearing jeans that seemed a smidgen tighter than they'd been earlier, and a tank top that, once again, accented his rounded biceps and his pectorals. But it was the hair covering that chest that stopped her. She had always loved hairy chests. Anthony's had been hairy...it had almost been her downfall. But Dusty's was thicker.

She tore her eyes from his chest and saw that he was having a little trouble tearing his eyes from her. "I should have worn my Born To Boogie T-shirt. I love the BoDeans, you know."

"Really?" he asked. He dropped the spatula he'd been holding and, throwing the dish towel over his shoulder, pulled her against him. "Let's see if you really were born to boogie."

She laughed as he moved her around the floor, dipped her and spun her. Then, pulling her close, he pressed his mouth against her ear and whispered, "You look great in that sweater, and you know it, don't you?"

She pulled back, feeling her cheeks reddening, and made herself look up at him. "This old thing?"

He let her go, shaking his head, and took in the sight of her tight leggings. "The pants don't hurt matters any."

She glanced down at the tight spandex on her legs. "You don't like my leggings?"

"I like them a lot," he said. "Too much."

"Good." She grinned and strolled over to the potatoes he had been washing. Grabbing a fork, she began puncturing them for the microwave. "Then we're even for the tank top." She gave him a sidelong glance. "You do have a great chest, you know."

"I was just thinking the same thing about you."

Grinning, she put the potatoes in the microwave, set the timer and turned back to him. "So, what are we gonna do while the steaks are cooking?"

"We're going to go over the map of Yazoo County and discuss the farms that I spray."

"Great," she said. "I thought I was going to have to handcuff you to get that kind of cooperation."

"Hmm," he said, intrigued. "Too bad I'm making it so easy."

She shot him a look. "So why are you?"

"Tomorrow I'll be flying at daybreak," he said. "And if you want to keep my customers, you have to know something about what they need from us."

"What do you care if we keep them?" she asked. "It's my problem now."

"You pay me by the load," he said. "That means it is my problem if we start losing business. And with the change of ownership, Sid and Gord are going to be using everything they have to get the rest of my customers."

"Sid and Gord Sullivan?" she asked. "I went to school with them."

"Yeah, well, get ready. As competitive as they were in football in high school, they're worse now. Sid's the one who worked for me, let me teach him everything he knows, then left and stole all my customers when I was in the hospital."

"The Sullivans, huh? Gosh, I graduated with Sid. I haven't seen him in over ten years. Maybe I'll pay him a visit tomorrow."

"A visit? Are you crazy? He's a viper. You can't go palling around with him and expect to compete."

"Who said I'd pal around with him? If I'm going to get your customers back, I have to know something about him. Find out where his Achilles' heel is."

"And you think you can get him to show it to you?"

"Hey," she said with a grin. "Don't underestimate my persuasive powers. I can come across like a weak little lamb, but at a moment's notice I can turn into a tiger. Besides, he remembers me as a flake. He'll drop his guard if he thinks I'm some dumb blonde.''

Dusty narrowed his eyes and studied her, thinking how he'd never consider her a dumb blonde. A reckless one, perhaps, or a frivolous one, or an impulsive one. But never dumb.

The microwave chimed, and she rotated the potatoes. ''So tell me something,'' she said. ''How did a crop duster get a name as obvious as Dusty, anyway?''

Dusty chuckled. ''My dad was an ag-pilot. One of the pioneers. What else would he name his kid?''

She smiled. ''Were you the only child?''

He shook his head. ''No, I have an older sister named Aggie.''

''Figures.''

He smiled. ''My sister Lilly got lucky, though. When she came along, Aggie and I talked him out of it.''

''Lilly Webb,'' Cindy said, looking up at him, suddenly serious. ''I went to school with her.''

He turned around. ''You knew her?''

''Yes,'' she said. ''We were in the fourth grade together, and the year she died I had her in several classes.'' Compassion darkened her eyes, and she couldn't help the emotion crossing over her face. ''I've never forgotten her, Dusty. Something about her death changed me, I think.''

His eyes were reflective as he set down his knife and focused on her. ''I don't remember you being one of her friends.''

"Well, I wasn't, really. At least, we didn't hang around together. But when she died..." She crossed the floor and looked up at him. "I think I realized how fragile and short life is. That if someone so sweet and so pretty and so young could die...that I could too. I guess I kind of took it as license to run amok. My parents had a lot of trouble with me after that. But it was my first experience with death."

"Mine, too," he said softly.

"Yeah." Her word was whispered, and she took his hand. "I'm so sorry, Dusty. I didn't know you were her brother."

"It's okay," he said. "It's been a long time."

"Yeah. But you know, I don't think there was a person in that school, whether they knew her or not, who wasn't affected in some way by her death. Some got religious, others got depressed...I guess I just started trying to defy death and live life as fast and as full as I could."

"I learned an apprecation for life I hadn't had before, too," he said. "Lilly really suffered at the end. And when she was gone..." His voice faded off, and he opened the oven and checked the steaks.

"You all suffered," Cindy said.

"Yeah. That's why it's so hard for me to understand your parents' attitudes. They have another chance with their child. Why can't they take advantage of it?"

"They're punishing me." She sighed. "They've never understood my divorce. They just think I got bored and decided to bail out. And I guess it's just as well that they believe that.''

Dusty gazed at her a moment. "What really happened?''

For a moment, Cindy thought she could tell him. But once again, she felt her face growing hot, felt the shame pushing up in her chest, felt the anger pounding in her heart. That door that had begun to open for him slammed shut, and she turned away. "It just didn't work out.''

"Why not? *Did* you get bored?''

Her eyes were misty as she turned back to him. "For your information, as much as I like to enjoy life, I consider marriage one of the most binding commitments in life. Boredom would never have driven me away. I would have just made it exciting.''

"What did, then?''

She shook her head. "It doesn't matter. It's over. I've built a lot of bridges since then, and I don't have to think about all that. I think the potatoes are ready.''

Dusty watched her as she opened the microwave and checked the potatoes, and he wondered what secrets she hid, what secrets that she couldn't even tell her parents to make them understand. There was pain in her eyes, pain of loss, pain of heartbreak. He knew that pain, for he'd felt it himself.

"So are the steaks," he said, pulling them out of the broiler. "Let's eat.''

For the rest of the meal, they bantered about the flying squirrel they saw fly down onto his porch, about Moon-baby and Dog the cat. But there was no more mention of death or divorce, heartbreak or loss. And he found that he liked light much better than darkness in her eyes.

When the meal was over, they spent two hours going over the map and marking who owned what land, and what was going to be planted where, what had already been defoliated, whose customers were Dusty's, and so on, until Cindy reached the saturation point and cried uncle.

He walked her out to her car, and noted the way the moon shone on her hair. Her eyes were bright and alive, even at night, and he thought how they'd lifted his spirits every single time he'd ever looked into them.

"I had a good time," she said lightly. "The meal was great. So was the company."

He smiled. "I liked the company, too. Even if she did buy my company out from under me."

"Hey, somebody had to do it. I may have kept you from having to work for Sid."

"Over my dead body." He looked at her for a long moment and told himself for the thousandth time that she was beautiful. A vision.

He stepped forward, instinctively wanting to kiss her, but something stopped him. "So you'll be there at daybreak?"

She smiled. "Have to. I live there, remember?"

"Can you get up that early?"

"I don't need a lot of sleep," she said. "I'll probably be up before you will."

"There's no television over there," he said. "You want to borrow a radio or something?"

"No thanks," she said. "Television makes me restless. I have trouble sitting still for very long."

"It's good company on a quiet night."

"Yeah, well. I enjoy my own company," she said with a grin.

He returned that smile. "I don't blame you."

Smiling, she got into the car, cranked it up, then rolled down the window. "You want to make a bet?"

"What?"

"About the business. I'll bet you that by the end of the summer, I'll have gotten all of your customers back from Sid, and then some."

"Never happen," he said. "I'll take that bet. What will I win?"

"You name it," she said.

He grinned and leaned in her window, his face much too close to hers, but she didn't show her discomfort. "If I win, I want a night when neither of us says no to the other. About anything."

She smiled. "That's what *I* plan on winning."

Her eyes danced with mischief as she began to back her car away, and grinning, he watched as she drove out of sight.

Chapter Seven

Cindy was buried in a heap of paperwork in his—her—office, when he got to the hangar at daybreak the next morning. The fact that she was going through his files riled him, but he didn't say anything. What was there to say, after all? She'd bought it all, lock, stock and barrel.

As he was digging through a stack of files for his logbook, Cindy glanced up at him. "Something wrong?"

"Nope," he said. "Just thinking about the work I have lined up."

"There's a list over there on the file cabinet," she said. "I thought you should probably start with Mr. Malone, since he called first."

Dusty scanned the list, then shot her a disgusted look. "I can't do Malone first. The way you've got this set up, you have me changing chemicals every other load."

She dropped her pencil. "Well, how would you do it?"

"I'd do all the farms needing the same chemical first. And I'd plan them out geographically." He pointed to her list. "It's stupid to have me going to the Malone place, then ten miles away to the Stegall field, then back up to the Simpsons' south thirty. That wastes time and fuel."

"Fine. Then you plan it out."

He slapped his forehead sarcastically. "What a great idea! Since I've done it every day since I've been in business, maybe I should!"

"Hey, Dusty, you don't have to get ugly. I was just trying to help."

"I don't need your help, Cindy. I'm the chief pilot here. I may not have another frigging thing to do with this business, but as chief pilot, I call the shots on what and when to spray."

"Fine." She sat back in her chair and gave him a look that spoke of too much authority. "There's enough there to keep you busy for most of the day, without my help. So after I finish studying the books, I'm going around to some of the customers, just to introduce myself and spread a little good will."

"Aw, hell," he said. "Please don't go around dressed like that."

She looked down at the cutoff shorts and Born to Boogie T-shirt she was wearing. "They're farmers, and I've known most of them since I was born! What's wrong with what I'm wearing?"

"They won't take you seriously. They'll flirt with you and joke with you, and then when you leave they'll laugh about the little blonde who's taking over Dusty Webb's life.''

"Oh, I see. It's an ego thing. You're afraid I'll embarrass you."

"Well, *look* at yourself!" he shouted. "I sold out to a woman who could pass for a Playboy Bunny!"

She smiled and preened her hair. "Well, thank you, Dusty."

His face reddened and he punched the air with his closed fist. "They don't want some Playboy Bunny spraying their crops! They'll like you enough to make lewd comments behind your back, and they'll fantasize about you when they're making love to their wives, but they will not—I repeat, will not—hire you to spray their crops. And if I know the folks around here, they may not want to hire me anymore, either!"

"Give me a break!" she returned, coming to her feet. "I am a businesswoman, and if I have to dress like one, that's fine. I can hold my own with farmers and diplomats alike, and I'd be willing to bet I'm already one of the best pilots in the state. I have as much right as you to run a business in this county, and I'll do it the way my instincts tell me I should!"

"By using your sexuality? By flaunting your legs? I'm telling you, baby, it'll get you somewhere, all right, but not where you want to be."

"Fine, then I'll wear what I had on last night at your house."

He flung around, clutching his head with both hands. "Damn it, you don't get it, do you? Last night you looked even better! You can't strut into these farmers' homes looking like a sexpot! Their wives won't let you in the door!''

Cindy sat back in her chair. "I think I may have just been paid a compliment, but somehow it seems like I've been insulted at the same time."

He shook his head and started for the door. "Do what you want. It's your business."

"Dusty!" She came around the desk, and he reluctantly turned back to face her. "I know this is hard for you. You've run this business successfully for fifteen years, and it wasn't your fault you had an accident and had to sell out. I'm trying to be considerate of all that. But I did buy it, and I have my own way of doing things. I won't embarrass you or myself. I may look like some kind of bimbo to you right now, but I can put on a little class when I want to."

His hard expression softened by degrees as he assessed the hurt on her face. Funny, he thought, that a woman with such a devil-may-care attitude could actually be so vulnerable at the whip of his sharp tongue. "Class?" he asked finally. "Lady, you've got it dripping from you. I never said you didn't have class. And I didn't say you look like a bimbo."

Her voice softened at his turnaround, but her cheeks still burned. "Should I cower away and not do my best at this, just because I'm a woman?"

"No, of course not."

"Should I pull my hair back in a ponytail, wear a pair of glasses with pop bottle lenses and blacken a tooth, just so they'll take me more seriously?"

His mouth cracked the slightest hint of a smile. "No."

"How about I just be myself? Truth is, that's the only way I know to be, Dusty. I can't play it any other way."

"Can you play it in long jeans and a less frivolous T-shirt?"

She smiled. "You got it. When I come down, I'll look like a schoolmarm on her day off. A blond schoolmarm . . . with an attitude."

Despite himself, he almost laughed. "Right. I meant it about the potato sack, you know. You'd look sexy as hell even in that. It's a curse you're going to have to live with." Her sweet smile made him uncomfortable, so he tried to regroup. "Look, just emphasize to each of them that I'll still be doing most of the flying and spraying. Let them know that not that much will change."

"I'll tell them you'll be doing half of the flying. But I won't make them think I'm staying on the ground, Dusty. That would be a lie."

"I'm not saying to lie. I'm just saying you have to ease them into this a little at a time."

"Trust me. I know what I'm doing."

Sighing, he threw up his hands and started out. "I have to go load the plane. Just do as little damage as possible, okay? Oh, and it might be better if you take my truck. That Porsche is a little flashy. Most of our farmers don't like to know we drive more expensive cars than they do. It makes them think they're paying us too much."

Cindy rolled her eyes. "Give me a break. I drive what I drive. They'll get used to it."

Cindy went back to her chair and plopped down as Dusty left the hangar.

CINDY WOULD HAVE DIED before she'd let him know it, but before she went to meet with the farmers, she agonized over each outfit she thought of wearing. A dress was too formal, she thought, but Dusty was right—shorts were too casual. She needed to portray efficiency and seriousness, yet friendly approachability. Finally, she settled on a pair of baggy jeans and a white blouse. Around her neck, she hung a bolo tie, and she secured her hair in a bun.

Too severe, she thought, pulling her hair back down. She'd just leave it loose. Dressed this conservatively, she'd have to at least leave herself one concession to her free spirit.

She watched Dusty circling overhead as she pulled her Porsche out onto the street and started up the road. Smiling, she waved up at him, but he didn't acknowledge seeing her. Somehow, she knew he had, and that he was still brooding. But that was okay. She didn't mind proving herself to him or anyone else. That, after all, was what she had come back here for.

FROM HIS PLANE, Dusty watched Cindy's car pull out of the driveway of the fifth farmer she had seen that day. This one had walked her out to her car and stood there talking to her for over an hour, before she'd driven away.

He dipped the plane and made a pass over the field he was defoliating, taking care to fly as low as possible to avoid any drift off of the target. He dreaded getting back to the hangar and checking the messages. Already, he'd probably had calls from all five farmers telling him thanks but no thanks, that they liked doing business with Dusty, but this little hellion wasn't quite what they had in mind. Then they'd probably add some lewd comments about her body, comments he'd already invented in his own mind, and suggest jokingly that he was sleeping with her... or trying to.

They'd get a lot of mileage out of this, and he was sure he'd never live it down.

He finished spraying his load and turned back toward the hangar, scanning the roads below him for Cindy's car. Where would she go next?

He watched her turn up the highway leading out of town toward the Sullivan Brothers' Flying Service, and he felt his muscles tensing. Was she really going to visit them?

Damn, he thought, circling back toward his landing strip. She was crazy. Out of control. And all he could do was watch her destroy his business one brick at a time.

CINDY RECOGNIZED SID the moment she pulled up to the Sullivan hangar. He was the one with the bald spot in the shape of a beanie and the protruding gut that spoke of championship beer consumption and frequent fast food. Across from the hangar was a beat-up trailer, where he had parked his red Corvette with the naked Madonna doll hanging from the mirror, and his souped-up pickup truck with huge wheels that lifted it almost as high as an eighteen-wheeler.

He turned when he heard her door opening, and she waved and got out of her car. "Sid, do you remember me?" she asked, exaggerating what she had left of her Southern accent.

He grinned. "Cindy? Cindy Hartzell?"

"None other."

Laughing, he came toward her, opening his arms to embrace her, as if they'd been long-lost buddies. "I heard you were back in town, girl. Everybody's talkin'."

"I'll bet."

"I heard you'd bailed ol' Dusty out." His laughter was phlegmy, and she fully expected him to spit.

"And I heard you'd robbed him blind."

Again, he laughed, and she joined in, as if they were coconspirators in some ludicrous joke no one else understood.

"Aw, now. I didn't rob nobody. He couldn't take care of his customers, so they came to me."

As he spoke, he leaned over her, his breath smelling like day-old beer. She wondered if he drank while he flew. If he did, the FAA might be interested to know it. "Well, whatever the story is, it looks like we're gonna be competitors."

His wheezy laugh profaned the country quiet. "Honey, I don't think you know what you're gettin' into. Dusty's business is fallin' faster than an Ag Cat with a dead engine. He's not right, since his accident.''

"Not right?" she asked. "How do you mean?"

"In the head. He shouldn't even be flyin'."

Something tightened in her chest, and her muscles went rigid as she took a step back. "Is that what you're telling people?"

"Ain't tellin' 'em nothin' that ain't true. He shouldn't have even lived through that crash. You shoulda seen his plane. You can't go through a crash like that and come out right."

"He's as right as anyone I've ever met, Sid. I think you know that."

"Well, you just give him time. You'll see. He flies off the handle and goes haywire at the slightest procrastination...."

"You mean... provocation?"

"Uh... yeah, whatever."

She looked down at her feet, trying not to smile. "I haven't noticed anything like that. He seems very stable to me. He has an ego that won't quit, but then, most men do." She chuckled conspiratorially. "No offense, huh?"

He laughed again, then turned his head and spat. She bit her lip and told herself to be thankful that he'd had the grace to turn his head, because she'd just bought this pair of sneakers last week.

"Seriously, though," he said. "You and me need to sit down and have a serious one to one. This is a serious situation, you know. I'm serious."

Again, she smiled. "Well, you know, I was just thinking the same thing. Seriously. But I've already had lunch, and I really need to get back to the hangar."

"Then how about dinner?" he asked, as they began walking back toward her car. "Be like old times."

Old times? she thought. What old times? "Sid, you and I never had dinner before."

"Then I was a damn fool," he said. "'Course, I don't remember you lookin' quite so delectable before."

And I don't remember your breath smelling quite so bad, she thought. Instead, she said, "I'd love to have dinner with you."

He laughed that phlegmy laugh again, spat, then rubbed her on the small of her back. Stepping forward to put some distance between them, she said, "You can pick me up at Dusty's hangar at seven. How's that sound?"

"Sounds too good to believe." As she got into the car, he leaned in the window. "We're gonna have a good time, honey. You won't regret it."

"I'm counting on it," she said, forcing a smile. "See you at seven."

He stood there watching after her as she drove out of his sight. Shivering, she thought of the date she'd made with him and hoped that she could make it worthwhile. If she was lucky, she could find out what other lies he was telling about Dusty, so that she could counter them to the farmers who had left him so far.

As for his inevitable advances, she'd just have to go prepared. A can of Mace and a strategically placed fingernail file had worked wonders before. And if they didn't work, she always had the old standby throat lock that her brothers had taught her when she was growing up.

There was something to be said for growing up in a house full of men.

She heard an engine overhead and looked up to see Dusty's plane coming toward her. She reached up and waved, knowing he had seen her coming from Sid's place. In response, he descended closer, closer, and then, just as she almost ran off the road, he ejected a white puff of smoke.

She began coughing and waving the smoke away, and wished she'd kept the top up today. But in seconds she was out of the cloud, and Dusty was on his way to his strip.

He would brood, she thought, and snip, and when she told him she was going out with Sid, he'd start preaching and lecturing about being taken advantage of and being stupid. She couldn't blame him, she thought, because he didn't know her that well yet. But he was about to find out.

Sid Sullivan might get screwed tonight, all right, but chances were, he wouldn't know it for a few days.

DUSTY WAS RELOADING the plane when Cindy pulled back up to the hangar. He didn't look up, and for a moment she wondered if he'd heard her drive up. But as she drew closer, she realized he was angry.

"All right, what's wrong?"

He glanced back over her shoulder. "What gave you the idea anything was?"

"Smoking me out on the highway, for one thing. Either it was flirting or it was an act of defiance. Judging from your mood, I don't think it was flirting."

"Smart lady. What did you and Sid cook up?"

She smiled and crossed her arms. "Nothing but a dinner date."

He swung around. "You're going out with that SOB?"

"Yep. You have a problem with it?"

He turned off the hose and dropped it, his nostrils flaring as he faced her. "Hell, yeah, I have a problem with it. He's a snake. He's our biggest competitor and he's getting worse all the time. What could you possibly want to go out with him for?"

"Information," she said.

"About what? I already know what he charges. I can find that out from just about any farmer interested in saving a dime."

"About how he's luring those customers away, Dusty. It isn't charm, you know."

He shook his head and rewound the hose. "That's no mystery, either. Farmers don't like change. They left me when I was sick and now they don't want to change back."

"Suit yourself," she said. "Whatever you want to think. But tonight, I'm having dinner with him."

"Fine!" he shouted. "You want to fraternize with the enemy, then you'll deserve whatever you get! And don't come whimpering to me when you regret the day you ever got in a car alone with that jackass!"

"I'm a big girl, Dusty." Chuckling softly to herself, she started into the hangar. She was halfway up the steps when she heard the plane's engine revving, and Dusty taking off in a huff.

CINDY FOUND DUSTY in the office when she came down to wait for Sid, and as he logged his day's work into the books, he brooded and tried hard to ignore her.

Sliding her leather-skirt-encased hips up onto the desk, she leaned over toward him. "So how do I look?"

"I'm not the person to ask."

She grinned. "Who is?"

"I don't know. I'm busy."

She looked down at the paper he was writing on. "How many loads did you do today?"

"I'm not sure."

"Did you get it all done?"

"No. There's enough left for a full day tomorrow."

"I'll start flying in a couple of days. After I've taken care of getting us some more customers."

"We've got all we're gonna get this season. Trust me."

"No, you trust me. We're going to get back all the ones you lost."

He looked up at her, his eyes dull. "And how are you gonna manage that? You gonna ask Sid real nice? Sleep with him, maybe, if he'll promise to give you some of his business?"

She stood up and glared down at him. "Whatever you think about me, Dusty, I'm not that mercenary. And I'm also not promiscuous."

"Yeah, right."

"I haven't slept with you, have I?"

He didn't answer, just turned the page in his logbook.

"And since I've been back, can you name one person that I've allegedly been to bed with?"

"You've only been back a few days."

"Oh, yeah. Give me time, right?" She got her purse, slid it over her shoulder and went back to the door. "I'll wait for Sid in the hangar. Lock up when you leave, will you?"

He gave her a scathing look. "Do you really think you have to remind me of that?"

"Hey, I'm just trying to get some communication going here, okay?"

He glared down at the desk, and she noted the popping of his jaw. "You know, it wouldn't work, anyway. Just in case you think it will."

"What?" she asked, chagrined.

"He might strike some kind of bargain with you, but he won't keep it. If you sleep with him, don't expect anything to be different in the morning."

For a moment she only stared back at him, then finally she began to laugh. "You're really something, aren't you?'' Her laughter faded, and her cheeks red-dened with anger. "I'll see you later, Dusty."

When she had disappeared from the doorway, Dusty dropped his face into his hands. Damn it, he couldn't believe this, he thought. He couldn't quite decide what riled him so much. It wasn't as if Sid could steal away the owner of the business. Cindy was here to stay, whether he liked it or not.

He heard a car pulling onto the gravel outside, and he glanced out the window and saw Sid's Corvette. He heard Cindy's laughter and told himself that he hated her, that he hated all women who could prance around in leather skirts and legs that went on forever, and soft little angora sweaters that clung where they shouldn't... He hated the control that women had over men, and he hated that he was at her mercy in more ways than the physical. His very livelihood depended on her, and what was she doing? Going out to pal around with the biggest thorn he'd ever had in his side.

They drove away, and he leaned back, rubbing the temples that were just beginning to throb. It was going to be a long night, he thought, but he wasn't budging from this building until she was home tonight.

Chapter Eight

It didn't matter that Sid took Cindy to an elegant restaurant all the way in Jackson, or that he had dressed up and doused himself with some cologne that she wished she could identify so she'd make sure she never smelled it again. No matter how civilized or cultured he pretended to be, she kept thinking that any minute he'd turn his head and spit.

"Yeah, ol' Dusty's had a real run of bad luck in the last coupla years," he said. "I hate to see it."

Cindy sipped her glass of wine and set it down. "It could happen to any one of us. Accidents happen. It was just unfortunate that he didn't have people he could trust working for him at the time."

Sid gave her a half grin, half frown, as if he didn't know whether she was joking or not. "You don't mean me and Gordy? Cindy, we did what we had to do."

"You could have kept flying for him, just like you'd intended to do before his accident."

"Well, you know what they say—all's fair in love and business." He finished off his beer, and she stared at him, wondering if he actually believed *anyone* said that. "Besides, he got back a good bit of that work when he came back."

"Not enough, and you know it. And the lost season last year cost him everything."

"Well, that's just your good luck, ain't it?"

"Maybe."

He laughed, too loudly, drawing looks from other diners. "Seems to me like you owe me some gratitude."

She didn't respond to that, and as the waiter brought their entrées, her mind wandered back to Dusty, pouting in that hangar and imagining all sorts of lewd sex scenarios between her and Sid. He must take her for a fool, she thought, but even if she'd been the worst kind of nymphomaniac on a deserted island, Sid Sullivan would have no chance with her.

Sid reached across the table and took her hand, startling her out of her reverie.

"You know, Cindy, you were good-lookin' in school, but now you're about the pertiest thing I've seen in this state in years. And you got brains, too. I like that."

"Do you?" she asked with a gentle, unthreatening smile. "Even if it means my taking business away from you?"

He laughed and squeezed her hand. "Honey, you don't know these farmers. They ain't goin' nowhere."

"Then how did you lure them away?"

"I didn't lure 'em nowhere. It was obvious that Dusty'd never be right again."

She stiffened and withdrew her hand. "You mentioned that today. What exactly do you mean?"

"His forgetfulness. He's been known to spray crops with the wrong chemicals, or leave out three or four passes just to save time. A few of my farmers even hired him to do work that he charged 'em for, but he didn't do 'em."

She reached into her purse and pulled out the writing pad she'd brought with her. "Which farmers? I need to know."

"Well . . . now, I can't give you that information. It wouldn't be right."

"Did they confront Dusty?"

"Well, hell, I don't know."

"How did they know that he didn't spray or that he put the wrong thing down?"

"I don't know. All's I know is that they came to me and I was glad to get 'em. It's the American way, Cindy."

"I know all about free enterprise, Sid," she said. "But I haven't seen any evidence of Dusty's having any problems with his memory or anything else since I've been here. He seems very capable and competent."

"Well then, you ain't been here long enough. You better watch him, though. That's not a good investment you just made, Cindy. He's gonna drag you down with him."

He started to eat, and she turned her head to avoid watching the huge bites he crammed into his mouth. "I'll tell you another thing," he said as he chewed. "I wouldn't trust him to maintain that plane you'll be flyin'. It was his own fault he crashed, you know. He hadn't been keepin' that plane up. He's lazy when it comes to routine maintenance."

She brought her eyes back to his. "He washes the plane every day after he flies. The engines look like they're in excellent condition. He just had the mechanic out last week doing some maintenance."

"Well, he knew you was comin'. What do you expect?"

"No," she said, "he didn't know. And it would be pretty stupid to deliberately ignore what needs to be taken care of when you're putting your life at risk every time you fly."

"Hey, you said it," Sid said, sitting back and holding his hands palm up. "Dusty's stupid. He's lazy and he's not the most honest man that ever hit the county. Just watch your back, Cindy. I'd hate to see you lose all your folks' money."

She bristled. "That money's mine, Sid."

"Oh? Hmmm. I heard . . . Well, never mind."

"You heard that my parents had set me up?" She felt her face reddening, but she tried to laugh. "If my parents were going to buy me a business, do you really think it would be a crop-dusting business?"

He laughed. "Well, you've never been known to be all that conventional, have you? I just thought they'd finally accepted it."

She looked down at her food and decided not to honor Sid with any more discussion about her family. "Let's get back to Dusty. I'm going to reserve judgment until I see for myself. I never take the word of others about a person's character. If people did that about me, I wouldn't have a friend in the world."

"You'd have me," he said with a lecherous grin.

She took a bite and looked across the restaurant, wondering if the disgust she felt showed on her face. He wasn't ready to let her off the hook.

"You really are perty, you know that?" he asked. "Has Dusty come on to you yet?"

She took a drink and lowered her lids as she brought her gaze back to him. "You tell me. Your grapevine seems pretty efficient."

"Dusty likes his women," he said on a chuckle. "Especially blondes. You're better lookin' than most of the gals I've seen him with lately, but he seems to go for the cheap type. You know. Big knockers and lotsa eye makeup."

"Oh, really?"

"Yep. You know why he's never married? It's because he's so addicted to that physical need of his that he can't settle on one woman. No one woman could ever satisfy somebody with a appetite like his."

She stiffened. "And what about you, Sid? Why didn't you ever marry?"

He shrugged. "Never met the right person." He touched her hand and grinned. "Not yet, anyway."

She pulled her hand away. "You know, for some-body who doesn't think much of Dusty, you sure have spent a lot of time tonight discussing him."

"That's just to help you out, honey. Show you what you've got yourself into. I hope I haven't upset you."

She breathed a laugh. "Upset? Why would I be up-set?"

He cleaned the last morsel off his plate and waved for the waiter. "You know, since I seen you this after-noon, I been contemplating what I could do to help you. And I think I've come up with a solution that might help both of us."

Cindy set her chin on her palm. "I'm listening."

"It has to do with us mergin'." She laughed, and he held out a hand to stop her. "Now just listen. You and me could wrap up this whole area. It would be prac-tically a monopoly. If we could get Dusty out of the picture, it could all be ours."

"What good would it be to have me join you? You'd have to split the profits with me. We might as well keep things like they are."

"But think," he said. "Right now, the overhead is outrageous. We'd only have to have the overhead for one business, and we'd have twice the work."

She frowned. "So let me get this straight. I get rid of Dusty..."

"You're the boss," he said. "Fire him."

"I see," she said. "I fire Dusty and close down our hangar and move in with you and Gordy. We com-bine all our customers and divide the profits three ways."

"Well, more or less. And instead of you comin' to our hangar, it would be more sensible for us to move in over at Dusty's hangar. It's set up for three planes already, and ours only holds one. Besides, his strip is a little better than ours...."

She smiled. "So you'd wind up with Dusty's entire business, without one cent of investment?"

"Well, no. You'd wind up with somethin', too."

She cut her steak and pretended to think a moment. "Tell me something, Sid. Why didn't you just buy Dusty's business when it was for sale?"

"Well, I don't think he'd have sold it to me, but I didn't see much point in it, anyway. I figured if I just waited, I'd have all his business eventually, anyway. He wasn't gonna stay afloat much longer."

She ate for a moment, and he watched her.

"So, what do you say?"

She sipped her wine, then brought her eyes back to him. "I say that I'd have to be a fool to merge with you when it's just a matter of time before I have all your business back, anyway. I don't need to give up everything to make ends meet."

It wasn't the answer he expected, and that very confidence in his ability to persuade her spoke volumes about his opinion of her intelligence. "You're kiddin' yourself, Cindy. You don't strike me as a gambler."

"Well, I guess you don't know me that well."

"Just think about it, huh? You don't have to decide right now. But you wait too long and the season'll be well underway. And you'll be losin' money left and right."

She watched as he gobbled down his pecan pie, then averted her eyes again and let them drift over the other diners in the room. He was a real piece, she thought. But she was glad she had come tonight. Now she knew how he had gotten all of Dusty's customers to stay with him. He'd told them lies, implied that Dusty was incompetent, mentally deficient, and even hinted at brain damage. It was amazing.

And Dusty didn't have a clue about any of it. But if she knew him, and she thought she did, he wouldn't do anything even if he knew. She couldn't see him doubling back to all his customers and telling them that he *wasn't* brain-dead. And first thing tomorrow she would find out if Sid's allegations about his lying and forgetting were true. If a farmer existed who had been cheated by Dusty, she'd find him.

The ride home was nauseating, for there's nothing worse for a pilot than to ride as the passenger of another pilot. He drove just like a crop duster, cutting curves too sharply, skidding on turns and flying down the long stretch of highway to Yazoo City. She thought if she made it home, she would count up all her blessings and never drive fast again herself. But that was a promise she knew she couldn't keep.

"So, whadda you say we go to my place for a while? Drink a coupla beers, watch a video or somethin'?"

She shrugged. "I'm pretty tired, Sid. And I have to get up early tomorrow."

"I got *Basic Instinct*," he said, as if that would change her mind. "If you ain't seen it, it's perty hot."

"I've seen it."

"Me, too," he said, "but I bought it so's I could watch it over and over. 'Course, I never watched it with a fox like you." He glanced over at her. "I told Gordy he'd have to stay somewhere else tonight. He's stayin' over at our folks' house so's I could have the trailer to myself."

Astounded, she gaped at him. "Pretty presumptuous of you, wouldn't you say?"

"Not really," he chuckled. "You have sex written all over you, Cindy, and you know it. You're as needy as I am."

Her face reddened. "If I have anything written all over me, it's boredom, Sid. Take me home."

"I promise you won't be bored at my place."

She shook her head. "I mean it, Sid. I'm not going home with you."

He gave her a disappointed glance, then started to laugh. "Oh, I see. You're one of those who likes to do it on her own turf. Okay, then. We'll go to your place. That way you won't have to rush home in the mornin'."

"Sid, I'm not spending the night with you."

"All right then. I'll leave afterward. Don't make no difference to me."

She couldn't help finding his confidence amusing, so she shook her head and decided to keep her mouth shut until they got to the hangar. Then, after she was home in one piece, she'd send him on his merry way.

He pulled up onto the tarmac at her hangar, and she saw that the light was still on in the office and Dusty's car was still parked out front. Was he waiting up for her?

She turned to Sid. "I had a nice time, Sid, but you don't need to come in."

"What? I thought we had this all worked out."

"I know you did. But you were wrong."

He reached for her, trying to pull her close enough to smell some of his charm. "Is it because Dusty's here? He knows you're a red-blooded woman, Cindy. He probably assumes we've done it already."

"He can assume what he wants, just like you do," she said. "But I''m not interested in taking off my clothes for you or seeing you take yours off for me. In fact, Sid, the thought nauseates me. And I have a strong stomach."

She got out of the car, and he got out, too, and caught her as she came around the front. Grabbing her, he said, "Tough lady, huh? All right. I like it. I can play it that way."

"Not with me, you won't," she said. "Sid, go home. I am not going to sleep with you, and I'm not going to merge my business with you. I'm not going to send you any business or roll over and play dead, and I'm not going to get tired of this and run off next week. You've met your match with me."

He dropped his hands from her arms and stared at her as if he couldn't believe his ears. "I thought you had a good time. I thought you intended to—"

"There you go with those assumptions again," she said. "I'll tell you what I intend to do, Sid. I intend to encourage Dusty to sue the pants off you for defamation of character, slander and whatever else my lawyer can come up with, if you keep spreading lies about him. And I intend to go to all of your customers and find out what you've told them already to keep doing business with you. And I intend to run you out of business by the end of the summer and watch you sell out to me. That's what I intend to do."

Even in the darkness, she could see his face reddening. "You think you can outsmart me, do you?"

She smiled. "It wouldn't be that hard, Sid, but frankly, I think all I'll have to do is sit back and watch. You'll do it to yourself."

She started to walk in, but he grabbed her arm and turned her back around. She jerked away from him. "If you value your manhood, Sid, don't ever touch me like that again. You may have heard I have a bad temper."

"All I've heard is that you're crazy."

"Believe it," she said. "And you just never know what a crazy person might do."

She stood stock-still as he cursed, got back in his car and skidded as he pulled off the gravel. Then, finally, she took a deep breath and went in the front door, near the office.

A soft lamp shone from the office, and she glanced in to see Dusty working on the same logbook he'd been working on when she left. Somehow, she doubted he'd been at it all this time. "Hi."

He looked up, as if he hadn't noticed she'd come in. "You back?"

"Yeah," she said. "Did you wait here for me?"

"No," he said. "I was just finishing up. I'm about to leave."

She shrugged. "Okay. Well, I guess I'll go on up." She started to walk away.

"So did you use protection?"

She flung around, suddenly as irate at him as she'd been at Sid. "Excuse me?"

"Did you take protection?" His eyes were blazing as he focused on her.

"Yes, as a matter of fact. A can of Mace and a fingernail file, neither of which I had to use since my greatest weapon is my mouth!"

"I'll second that."

She dropped her purse and went into the office, sank down into a chair and crossed her arms. "All right. Just get it all out, Dusty. You've obviously got something on your mind."

"I just can't figure it out, Cindy. I mean, I know you contend that you're trying to get secrets out of the enemy—that would fly for a business lunch or a nice afternoon chat—but this dating stuff between you and Sid...it's like putting Julia Roberts with Don Knotts."

"Is that supposed to be another of your offhanded compliments?"

"No! I just don't get it. He's the most lecherous, low-down redneck scumbag you could find in this town, not to mention the number-one threat to this operation!"

"Exactly," she said, getting to her feet. "Which is why I subjected myself to this so-called date in the first place, a fact that you would realize if you weren't wrestling with your own jealousy!"

"Jealousy? You've got to be kidding."

Cindy set her hands on her hips and glared at him across the desk. "Then you explain your reaction. All night I've been listening to him tell me how you're brain damaged, incompetent and kinky, and now I come home to this? I should have kept my mouth shut and not defended you. I'm going up to bed."

She was halfway across the hangar when Dusty caught up with her. "Defended me? I don't need anybody defending me! I haven't done anything!"

"You don't have to do anything. All he has to do is plant those seeds of doubt in your farmers' minds, and they're his."

"What seeds of doubt?"

She set her hands on her hips and squared off with him. "All right. For starters, that you'd ruined some of their crops by spraying the wrong chemicals."

"That's a lie. If I'd done that, they would have sued me."

"And that you had charged for work you'd never done. That you had memory lapses, raging temper tantrums..."

"That son of a—"

"That's pretty much what I thought, Dusty, until you flew off the handle at me just now. Maybe that part of his characterization of you was true, huh?"

She started up the stairs and slammed into her apartment before he could say another word.

Collapsing onto a chair, she kicked off her shoes and raked her hair back from her face. Damn them, she thought. Damn them all. There wasn't a person alive that deserved the kind of hassles she'd been through tonight.

She heard a knock on the door and, not getting up, she threw a look in that direction. "What?"

"Let me in," Dusty said. "I want to talk to you."

"I'm through talking," she said. "Go home."

"Not until you let me in. Come on, Cindy. Let's be adults about this."

"Adults?" She got up and threw the door open, and he pushed inside. "I'm not the one acting like a child, Dusty."

"You're right." He turned back to her and closed the door. "I'm sorry."

"You're . . . what?"

"I'm sorry. I shouldn't have lambasted you that way, but I just sat there all night, thinking about your being out with him . . ."

She felt her anger subsiding, and a soft smile tugged on her lips. "That sounds a little bit like jealousy to me."

His chest moved up and down with heavy breaths as he stood staring at her. "Not jealousy. Just reality."

"And what, pray tell, is that reality?"

He grinned slightly. "That you're a fantastic-looking woman with a body that most models would kill for, and that Sid Sullivan's probably never in his

life been out with anyone like you. I didn't think he'd
let the opportunity pass."

His words hit her between the eyes, and she couldn't
quite find a clever quip to return. It wasn't the time for
sarcasm, and suddenly that awkwardness pushed up
inside her. That old protective alarm that told her not
to get too close. She tried to think of something to
come back with, something to lighten the moment, but
before her mind could grab anything, he came toward
her, his big body towering above her. Suddenly she felt
very small, very vulnerable, very confused.

"Did he?"

"No," she whispered. "He gave it his best shot. I'm
just not as easy as the scuttlebutt says I am."

"I know you're not."

She could feel his breath on her face, smell the pep-
permint he always seemed to have in his mouth, the
slight soapy smell that told her he'd been home long
enough to shower tonight.

"But easy or not," he rumbled, "you have something about you that can keep a man awake nights.
Maybe you don't even realize it."

She swallowed and started to step back, but before
she could, he set his big rough hands on her shoulders.

"You're making me crazy, you know that?" he
whispered. "Tonight, when I kept picturing you with
him, I came as close to snapping as I'll ever be."

She could feel his heart pounding against her breast,
felt his legs emanating heat against hers. "Dusty,
I—"

"What?" he whispered.

She looked up at him to answer, but the thought vanished as his mouth descended slowly to hers.

The moment their lips came together, she felt that old desperate craving swell up inside her. His kiss took her higher than she'd ever gone by plane, banished every thought except that of getting closer to him.

Her heart pounded out of control, and when he broke the kiss and dropped his lips to her neck, she arched her back and moaned softly. His hands drifted up through her hair and his lips came back to hers again.

Five years ago, in this same position, she would have gone with it, surrendered to the chemistry smoldering between them. But she'd learned too many hard lessons since then.

Slowly, she pulled out of his kiss. Her breath was telltale heavy as she looked up at him with wide, smoky eyes.

"Wow," she whispered.

"Wow what?"

"Just...wow." She stepped back, putting some distance between them. "Your...technique is a little more effective than Sid's, I'll have to admit, but—"

"Technique?" He grinned and stepped closer. "It's no technique, Cindy. None of this is planned. There's something here, and you know it."

"Yes, I do. I won't deny that." She turned away, straightened her hair and tried to stop the trembling in her hands. "It's just...I'm not like you think I am."

"Not passionate?" he whispered, coming up behind her. "Not feminine? Not beautiful?"

"I'm not promiscuous. I can't sleep with people I've only known a few days."

"Why not?"

"Because, as frivolous as I may seem to you, I get attached, Dusty. To all the wrong men. To men who don't deserve it. There's too much at risk."

For a moment, he stood still, staring at her. "Somebody's done a number on you, Cindy. Who was it?"

"Nobody. I just—"

"Your husband?"

She slid her hand through her hair and looked up at him. "I don't want to talk about it."

"What did he do? Cheat on you?"

Her eyes shot to his.

"Is that it? You loved him and he cheated on you?"

She issued a mirthless laugh and turned away. "It's hardly cheating when they don't do a whole lot to hide it."

"It still hurts."

"How do you know?" She brought her hardening eyes back to his. "Have you ever committed your life to someone and had it thrown back in your face?"

"No. But I can see the hurt in your eyes, as much as you try to hide it."

Her eyes filled with tears, for the first time in over a year. She never cried; tears diminished life, she told herself. There was too much to laugh about.

It was just that she couldn't find anything right now.

She started for the door and he stopped her. "Where are you going?"

"To take the plane out," she said. "I feel like flying."

"At night? You can't fly at night. There are no lights on the strip."

She hesitated, then went into the kitchen. "All right. Never mind."

He followed her. "Is that what you do when you start to hurt? Go do something reckless? Squeeze out a little adrenaline to fight the depression?"

"I'm not depressed!" she said. "I've never been depressed in my life."

"Not even when your husband betrayed you?"

"I told you. It's not betrayal when he doesn't even try to hide it. I betrayed myself. I never should have married him."

"So you're determined never to fall for anyone again?"

"I never say never, Dusty. I don't know what I'll do. But I'm not sleeping with you or anyone else just because you want me to."

"What about what you want?"

She threw her face up and faced him directly. "Wanna know what I want, Dusty? I want you, all right. And if I were a different person, we'd be rolling around on that bed right now, probably having the best sex that either of us has ever had. But then tomorrow we'd have to wake up and face the day, and you'd start wishing you'd never gotten that intimate with me, and I'd start wishing I didn't expect some emotion to be involved. And the only thing I hate worse than boredom, Dusty, is regrets."

He stood there staring at her for another moment and, finally, he strode across the room, and put his face close to hers again. As he looked down at her, she told herself that if he pushed it much further, she wasn't sure she was strong enough to turn away.

Instead, he stroked a hand through her hair, pressed a kiss on her forehead and tipped her face back.

His kiss was soft, gentle and absolutely disarming, and when he broke it, she kept her face up and her eyes closed. But Dusty only whispered, "I don't want you regretting anything, Cindy. I'll see you tomorrow."

Cindy didn't move as Dusty kissed her one last time, then left her apartment.

Chapter Nine

This isn't working out, Dusty thought as he lay in bed that night, staring at the ceiling and trying to forget how much he'd wanted Cindy tonight. If he had been able to sleep with her, maybe some of the frustration wouldn't be so strong, he thought. But since he hadn't, he was building her up into some kind of fantasy figure in his mind, making her into something she could never live up to in a million years.

He had to get her out of his head.

He sat up and told himself that it wasn't doing him any good to focus on her so much. What he needed was to see somebody else, someone who could get his mind off her. Someone more practical, who wouldn't cost him quite so much.

He picked up the telephone and dialed the number of a woman he'd been out with several times, and dropped his head back onto the pillow as she answered. "Hey, Bev. How's it going?"

"Dusty! You devil, you haven't called me in a week!"

"Been busy. Listen, you wanna have dinner tomorrow night? We could go to the steak house. . . ."

"Why don't you let me cook for you instead?" she asked. "I've got some hens that need to be eaten. Besides, it's too short notice to get a baby-sitter for little Janie. I could put her to bed early and we could be alone."

"Sounds good," he said.

They set the time for six-thirty, since that would enable him to make an early evening of it, and when Dusty hung up, he dropped his head back against the pillows. Damn, he thought. He didn't really want to eat dinner with Bev tomorrow night, or listen to the fits her spoiled little daughter threw whenever she didn't get her way. He would rather eat hamburgers on the floor of the hangar with Cindy.

But Cindy didn't appear to be interested.

He closed his eyes and told himself that he couldn't keep torturing himself any longer. Bev was a nice-looking, good-natured woman, and there was nothing wrong with her.

The problem was that there was just so much right with Cindy.

CINDY SPENT THE BETTER part of the next morning paying visits to all of the customers that Sid had stolen from Dusty and asking them, point-blank, why they had stayed with Sid after Dusty came back.

Two of them admitted that he'd convinced them that Dusty couldn't handle the job anymore, and that he had already destroyed several cotton fields and couldn't keep his books straight.

"Why didn't you hear about a lawsuit if he screwed things up?" she asked them each.

One of them had shrugged and offered the definitive answer. "They settled out of court. Kept it quiet."

"It didn't happen," she had argued, "and if you don't believe me, you can just get on the phone with every farmer in the county and ask them. Don't you think you'd have heard if someone around here lost an entire crop?"

"Well, Sid said it happened. I figured whoever it was was tryin' not to ruin Dusty."

"Sid lied to you. That's the only way he could get your business. And now I'm going to use some underhanded means to get it back," she said. "I'm going to offer you a special if you come back right now. For every hundred acres you let Dusty or me spray, I'll give you five acres free. And this month our prices are already lower than Sid's."

The farmer had frowned. "If I find out Sid lied to me, I'd go back to Dusty. But to be perfectly honest, I don't know about you. Spraying defoliant can be pretty hairy sometimes. If the wind blows, it can kill off trees and get in people's yards...or cross over into crops I've already planted. You need an expert for that."

"I understand your concern," she said. "And I'll promise you that I'll leave the defoliating to Dusty. But I can spray your wheat right now, and when you get your cotton and beans planted, I'll be able to handle that. Come on, just try us."

"Let me think on it," the farmer said, as had so many others that morning. "I'll get back to you."

She had finally gone back to the hangar feeling defeated and fatalistic. Then she listened to the messages that had come while Dusty was flying. One after another of the farmers she had spoken to put in enough orders to fill up the next day with both her and Dusty flying.

She heard his plane pulling up on the tarmac and she ran out, jumping up and down. "We did it! We got the business back!"

"What?" he asked as he climbed out of the cockpit.

"Look at all these orders!"

Dusty took the notebook from her hand, scanned it, then gave her a questioning look. "How did you do this?"

"I cleared up those rumors Sid had spread around about you, for one thing."

"They had believed him?" Dusty asked, astounded.

"Heck, yes, they believed him. And my guess is that the telephone lines have been buzzing all morning while they tried to find out how much of what they'd been told is true. And my special didn't hurt anything."

"Special? What kind of special?"

"For every hundred acres, they get five acres free."

"What? Are you out of your ever-loving mind?"

"It's just an introductory offer. They have to have an incentive for coming back, Dusty."

"But we'll go broke like that!"

"It's not your problem, Dusty. You'll still be making what we agreed on per load. And you'll have a lot more loads than you would have, even with me flying."

"Not if we go broke by July."

"We won't go broke. It's only for the next three weeks and then the prices will go back to normal. The trick is going to be getting to their work as soon as possible after they call. If they don't have to wait for us, and we're willing to work weekends and squeeze as much as we can get into each day, then by the time we're back on the same price scale with Sid, they'll prefer us, anyway. They did business with you for all those years before Sid came along. And now that they've found out he duped them, they might not look too kindly on him anymore."

He gazed down at the list of orders again, then pulled off his helmet. "Damn. I'll never get all this done."

"We're going to do it together," she said. "We can do it, Dusty. Of course, I can't defoliate. I promised a couple of the farmers that if they came back, you'd do all that. But I can fertilize the wheat now and spray the rice. There are a lot of orders on here for those." She gave a tiny jump and laughed aloud. "Say it, Dusty. I'm a genius."

He grinned. "That remains to be seen. But right now, we'd better get busy. Come on inside and we'll take a look at the map and decide which one of us will do what."

Still laughing, Cindy followed him inside.

CINDY WAS ALMOST FINISHED spraying the McCarty acres when Dusty radioed to her from the hangar. "Come in, Cindy."

"Yeah, Dusty?"

"I finished up with everything I was trying to do. I hate to leave you while you're still flying, but I've got to be somewhere."

"Oh, yeah?" she asked. "Where?"

His pause told her that she'd gone over her bounds, and she grinned.

"Just . . . out. I have plans. Over."

"A date, huh?" Something twisted in the pit of her stomach, but she tried to keep smiling. "Who's it with, Dusty?"

"Never mind," he said. "I'll be in my truck, so if you need me, you can radio me. But you don't have time for more than one more load before it gets dark. Over."

"I'm almost finished," she said. "We've got to hire somebody to work for us, Dusty. If we didn't have to load our own planes, we could save a lot of time."

"If you don't drive us into bankruptcy, maybe we can. Over."

"You'll have faith in me before you know it," she said. "Have fun with what's-her-name. And try to disregard the black roots in her hair. The two-inch nails probably make up for that, don't they?"

She could hear the grin in his voice. "Trust me. Her hair is just fine. And personally, I like the feel of those nails on my back."

Her smile faded and her cheeks burned hot. "You didn't say 'over.'"

"I know," he said. "I kind of got lost in thought there for a minute." She heard him chuckling, and then he said, "See you tomorrow. Over."

She hung her mike back on its brace and tried not to be so chagrined as she watched him pull away from the hangar, on his way to be with another woman. One who, no doubt, was more willing. One who probably didn't have redneck hair at all, but long silky hair that put hers to shame.

The thought made her ill, and as she landed, she told herself that it shouldn't matter. He meant nothing to her, anyway. What he did in his off time was none of her business.

If she could only stop thinking about it, she'd be all right. She had drawn the lines between them herself, after all.

"AND SO I TOLD HER that she could just priss right over there and tell that man what she'd done," Bev droned on as Dusty tried to look interested. "And she did. But she had these big ol' tears in her eyes, and the man couldn't work up any anger." Leaning her head back, she let go a laugh that he feared might wake the sleeping three-year-old on the couch. "Last time she ever shoplifts, I'll bet."

Dusty smiled and set his napkin on the table. "That'll probably keep her out of the penitentiary, Bev."

The woman accepted his sarcasm and began scraping the leftovers of his plate onto hers.

"So why are you so short tonight, babe?" the woman asked. "You tired?"

"Yeah," he grunted. "I guess so."

"Season's about to get busy," she said. "I'll probably never see you anymore."

"You know how it gets," he said.

"So tell me about that loony Hartzell girl. Has she caused any problems yet?"

He checked his watch discreetly, shaking his head as he did. "No, actually. She's gotten a lot of the business back. And she's a good pilot."

"Not as good as you, I'll bet." She got up and came to sit on his lap, and, as he usually did, he took her willingly. Dropping a kiss on his lips, she said, "I just don't know what happens to me when I watch you fly. I just get all . . . jittery inside."

"Oh, yeah?" He smiled as she began to unbutton his shirt and reach inside to stroke his chest.

"Yeah. Just thinkin' about it makes me kind of crazy. And you know what I like to do when I'm crazy?"

He tilted his face up to receive a long, wet, promising kiss, when through the open window he heard his radio blaring in his truck. Breaking the kiss, he tried to listen as Cindy read off his call number.

"Dusty? Come in, please, Dusty."

Dusty almost shoved Bev off his lap and dashed through the door and out to his truck, with the woman on his heels.

"What is it?" she asked as they ran.

"It's Cindy," he said, opening the door and grabbing his radio mike. "Come in, Cindy."

"Dusty, I've...uh...kind of got a problem."

He could hear the tension in her voice, and a tight sense of foreboding washed over him. "What kind of problem? Over."

"Well...uh...it's too dark, and I can't see the strip...."

His face reddened instantly, and he pressed the mike's button again. "Are you telling me you're still flying?"

"Yeah. I'm still up in the wild black yonder. I thought I could get one more load in before it got too dark to land. Miscalculated a little."

"Damn it, Cindy, you sure as hell did!" He got into the truck and slammed the door, yelling through the window, "I've got to go, Bev. She'll get herself killed if I don't figure out some way to light the strip for her. Thanks for supper."

"But, Dusty! Can't you come back after—"

"Not tonight, Bev," he said, pulling out as she ran along beside him. "See you later."

He turned his truck around and headed toward his strip as fast as he could.

The radio crackled again. "Dusty? Are you there?"

"I'm here," he said. "I'm on my way to the strip. I'm gonna have to get a few friends to come light it up with their headlights so you can land. Do you have any idea how asinine this is?''

"Some idea," she said facetiously. "I'm really sorry. I didn't think—"

"You didn't think. What an understatement." He turned a corner and his back wheels skidded. "How are you with fuel?"

"Fine," she said. "No problem there."

"Well, now all I have to do is think of some people who can help us without telling everybody and his brother that you just pulled one of the dumbest stunts known to man."

She was silent for a moment, then said, "All right, Dusty, you don't have to get mean about it. I've learned my lesson."

"So have I," he said. "Never to leave you alone with a plane. Over."

The radio crackled again, and finally she said, "Why don't you call my brothers? They each have trucks, and they won't tell because they'll be too embarrassed. But they'll come."

Dusty nodded. "Yeah. Not a bad idea."

"But not my father," she added quickly. "Don't tell my father or my mother."

He chuckled lightly. "Why not, Cindy? You afraid this'll prove to them that you're not competent to run a business as dangerous as this one?"

He could tell his words had cut her and, for an instant, wished he hadn't said it.

"Something like that," she returned quietly.

He hung the mike up and navigated his way through the back streets to the hangar. Just before he pulled onto the dirt road leading to it, the radio sizzled again.

"Dusty? Did I ruin your date?"

He breathed a heartless laugh. "Of course you did."

For a moment she didn't say anything, then finally she said, "Good. I guess there's a bright side to this, after all."

Despite his anger and irritation at her, Dusty couldn't help grinning as he brought his truck to a halt in front of her brother's house.

CINDY CHECKED HER FUEL gauge as she circled the hangar and told herself she had plenty. But she hadn't counted on it taking this long to get someone here to help her.

She saw a procession of headlights coming up the road toward the hangar, and when they turned onto the dirt road leading to Dusty's, she realized it was her brothers. But there was something wrong. Instead of three cars, there were five.

Had they gotten their wives to come, too? she wondered with a twist of apprehension. If so, who was with the children?

She pressed her radio button to ask the fateful question. "Dusty, come in."

"This is Dusty. Come in, Cindy."

"Why are there five cars coming to the hangar? Tell me it's not what I think. Not my parents."

"I couldn't help it, Cindy. It's hard to untangle one Hartzell from another. Two of your brothers were at your parents' house when I found them. I was more interested in hurrying than in keeping them quiet. Over.''

"Thanks a lot," she said. "But if it's all the same to you, I think I'll just fly until I run out of fuel and let myself fall where I may."

"Come on, Cindy, this is serious. We have to get you down. Wait until I get everybody lined up, and then I'll radio you when it's clear. Over."

Cindy gave a great sigh and watched as the cars began to drive down the strip and line up with their headlights shining on the narrow piece of dirt on which she was to land. It wouldn't be hard, she thought. The hard part would be getting out of the plane and listening to her mother lecture and her father lambaste her about her stupidity. Just like old times.

"All right, Cindy," she heard Dusty say, after the seven cars, including hers and Dusty's, were lined up on both sides of the strip. "Bring her on in."

She didn't even have the heart to answer. Circling back around, she began her descent, not at all nervous about touching down, but scared to death of seeing the contemptuous looks on her parents' faces. It was almost enough to make her do a nosedive into the ground. Almost... but not quite. Instead, she decided to show them the best landing she was capable of.

She came in smooth and gentle between the headlights, and her touchdown was so careful that she wouldn't have spilled a cup of coffee sitting on her knee. She brought the plane in to the tarmac and turned it around so it could easily be pulled into the hangar. As she pulled off her helmet and opened the door, she saw the cars coming like the cavalry to surround her.

Like Amelia Earhart at the end of her journey, she got out with a hero smile and waved her arm above her head.

Her father was the first one out of his car. "Are you crazy, girl?"

"Hi, Daddy. Thanks for helping me out." She hopped off the wing and pressed a kiss on his cheek.

"Your mother is a nervous wreck. Are you determined to send us all to Whitfield?"

She smiled at the reference to the state mental institution and turned to her mother, who was getting out of her Lincoln. "Hi Mom. How'd you like my landing?"

Her mother had been crying, and her hands still trembled. "Oh, Cindy!" She threw her arms around her daughter, then quickly thrust her away and turned back to her father. "Tell her, Hyram! Tell her what you told me."

Cindy braced herself as Dusty got out of his truck and came toward them, her brothers on his heels. "Tell me what?"

"Cindy, I'll give you back what you paid for this business, plus all the original amount of your trust fund for you to blow again to kingdom come, if you'll just stop this madness."

Cindy's smile faded. She glanced at Dusty, who had stopped cold on his way to the plane. He turned back. "Why? Why would you do that?"

"Because I'd rather see you drive me to bankruptcy than to kill yourself in that plane."

A soft smile tugged at her lips, battling with the daunting feelings of anger rising inside her. "That's some offer."

"He means it, Cindy," her mother said. "You've got to get out of this. If it's a job you want, you can go to work with your brothers. Or . . . you could go back to school. Anything—just stop this nonsense."

"Then . . . what would happen to Dusty's flying service?"

"Who cares?" her father shouted. "I could sell it to someone else. I don't know. The point is to get you out."

"But I've done some good things for the business," she said. "I'm a good crop duster, even if I do make a little mistake in judgment every now and then."

"A little mistake in judgment?" her father repeated at the top of his lungs. "A mistake in judgment in my business will cost me a hundred dollars. In yours, it'll cost you your life."

"Why now?" she asked, allowing her anger to take full control of her face. "Why wouldn't you give me the time of day before?"

"You didn't deserve the time of day before!" her mother said. "But now we realize that drastic measures have to be taken."

"Why?" she asked. "To keep me from embarrassing you further, or to get me back into the family because you love me?"

Her father's voice cracked as he shouted, "You're our daughter! Of course we love you!"

Dusty looked down and she could see the censure in his face. She dropped her eyes and looked at her sneakered feet, then brought her eyes back to her father. "Then you'll love me even if I'm a crop duster, won't you? And it wouldn't cost you another cent."

"Cindy, if you do what we say, you can have all that money and a home and a family again," her mother said. "But if you insist on keeping on with this nonsense, you can forget our ever taking you back in. You'll be on your own forever, and we'll forget we even have a daughter."

Cindy tried to smile. "You know, Mom, in some circles that's called emotional blackmail. And I'd rather crash and burn than to be manipulated back into a pretty prison where I have to toe the line. I came back here because I missed my home," she said. "But if my home isn't there, I'll just have to build one of my own."

Blinking back her tears, she went up to each brother, who had stood quietly, and pressed a kiss on their cheeks. "Thanks for helping me out, guys."

Jake pulled her back and gave her a serious look. "Hey, don't go flying at night anymore, okay? I was in the middle of a killer episode of 'Murphy Brown.'"

Smiling, she punched him. "Next time I have an emergency, I'll try to time it better."

She glanced at Dusty, who still stood quietly, watching her from the sidelines of her family playing field, and quietly she turned and went inside.

DUSTY WAITED UNTIL everyone was gone before he put the plane up, locked and secured the sliding doors of the hangar and turned off the lights. He thought of leaving, but somehow he felt the need to talk to her. Besides, she had no food in the apartment, and he could see that she was exhausted.

He picked up the phone and called for a pizza, then busied himself doing the final maintenance chores around the hangar while he waited for it. When it arrived, he climbed the stairs to her room and knocked softly on her door.

She opened it and peeked around the door. Her hair was wet, and the scent of soap and steam filled the apartment.

"Thought you might be hungry," he said. "Hope you like pepperoni."

Her smile was one of relief and gratitude. "Come in, Dusty."

He pushed the door open and went into the barren little room that he had expected her to have abandoned by now. Instead, she had managed to put her signature on it with a gigantic Australian wall hanging in the center of the room, boasting a lion, a hawk and a koala bear. He wondered which one represented her, then, smiling to himself, admitted she was all three. In her own way, she possessed the courage of the lion, the spirit of the bird and the heart of the bear.

When he turned back to her, he saw that she wore nothing but a towel.

His groin tightened, and he felt like a deer trapped by a set of unexpected headlights. "Did I get you out of the shower?"

"No," she said, taking the pizza from him as naturally as she would if she were fully dressed. "I'm starved. This is great."

His heart began to pound heavier, and as she opened the box and pulled out a piece, he wondered if she planned to make any attempt to get dressed.

Her shoulder still glistened with wetness, and, allowing his eyes to drop down to the swell of her breasts, he reached up and wiped some drops away.

Quickly, she stepped back. "Just because you caught me like this," she said, "don't get any ideas."

"Ideas?" He almost laughed, but suddenly realized this was very serious. "You're standing there wrapped in a towel, soaking wet and eating a pizza like I see you this way every day."

"Hey, you came up here. I didn't plan for you to bring me a pizza just as I was getting out of the shower."

"No, and you're still making no attempt to cover yourself up."

She grinned and took another bite. "So is it bothering you, Dusty? Is that it?"

His mouth went dry, and he willed his breathing to slow down. But there was no hiding the signs of his arousal. "I don't understand it," he said. "What is it you're looking for? Do you want me to beg? Cajole?

Or are you trying to see how far you can push me before I take you by force? Is that what turns you on, Cindy? A little macho insistence?''

The flip look on her face vanished, and she took a step back. "Are you threatening me?"

He laughed softly and shook his head. "No, Cindy. I'm not turned on by resistance. If you want me, you'll have to extend the invitation more directly."

She tossed the box of pizza at him and, with a half smile, started for the bathroom. "Here," she said. "Have a piece. I'm getting dressed."

He dropped into the chair as she closed the door behind her, and he willed his breathing to settle, and his heart to stop pounding, and the rest of his body to stop reacting to her wet, naked, towel-clad body.

Damn it, he thought. He had come up here to offer her comfort over her parents, thinking she was probably upset. And chances were, she had known he would.

So why this new turn?

Suddenly it hit him like a brick between the eyes. She had known he'd want to talk about her parents' attitudes, so she had diverted his attention. She didn't like his compassion or his sympathy, so she had effectively changed the subject.

Amazing, he thought. She was amazing. And now he sat there, filled with desire and no outlet, and he couldn't tear himself away. Being around her was like holding on to a ski boat that was pulling him through the rocks. It was a terrible thing, yet he couldn't let go. The thrill was more intense than the aggravation.

He tried to eat a piece of pizza so he'd look more relaxed and less aroused when she came out.

When she did, she was wearing a pair of yellow shorts and a soft yellow shirt tucked in. Her hair was still wet, but hung loosely down her back. She sat in the old recliner across from him, curling her feet beneath her, and reached for another piece of pizza. "Dusty, I'm really sorry I ruined your date."

He pushed aside the surprise that she'd apologize for that, rather than for flying after dark and causing such a panic. Still, he grinned. "Yeah, and I was about to get lucky."

"Were you now?" she asked, sniffing. "Well, gosh, maybe you should go back."

He smiled and shook his head. "Nah. The mood has passed." He held her eyes. "For her, anyway."

"It can be revived, I hear."

He laughed softly. "Jealousy really looks good on you, you know that?"

She gasped. "Jealous? What would I have to be jealous about?" She paused and gave him a wide-eyed look. "Is she pretty?"

"I don't date ugly women," he said.

"Is she sexy?"

He smiled. "Every woman is sexy in her own way."

"Bull dooky."

He frowned at her pseudocurse word. "Excuse me?"

"I said, bull dooky. You don't believe that for a minute. I guess the fact that she was willing more than made up for those black roots, huh?"

"She doesn't have black roots," he said. "Actually, she's a redhead."

"Bet it isn't real," she countered.

He smiled. "It is. Trust me."

Her face reddened, and she stared at him for a moment. Taking the chance to get a little control over the conversation, he asked, "So what do you think of your parents' offer?"

He noted the way she seemed to tense up as she dropped her feet and reached for another piece. "What do *you* think?"

He shrugged. "I don't know what to think. Would he sell out or let me run it for a while? And if he sold it, there's no guarantee I'd have a job. If I ran it, with all the business you've drummed up lately, I wouldn't be able to handle it all without you."

She sighed. "I thought you considered me more of a hindrance than a help."

He set his pizza down and leaned back, laughing with more frustration than he knew was possible.

"What's so funny?" she asked, smiling with him.

He shook his head and waited until he had control of his voice again. "Hey, anybody who can work so long in one day that they let the dark sneak up on them deserves some credit."

She smiled and took another bite. "I thought so."

"It's a lot of money, though," he whispered. "Maybe you should consider taking it."

As if she'd suddenly lost interest in eating, she dropped her slice back into the box. "I don't want it," she whispered. "I've had money. It didn't buy me what I wanted."

"And what was that?"

She looked over his head for a moment, seeing things he couldn't see, remembering things he had no knowledge of. "Belonging," she said. "And despite my family's attitude or the obstacles I've hit here, I do feel that I belong here. More than I ever have anywhere else."

"Maybe you just want it badly enough to imagine it," he said quietly.

She shook her head. "There's a smell here. The smell of green things growing. The smell of wildflowers and magnolias and honeysuckle. I can't find that smell anywhere else. And I can't wait until the cotton comes up and I can see miles and miles of that white, billowy stuff growing like clouds all around us. It's home, Dusty, and no matter what I ever have or where I ever go, and no matter who turns their back on me, it will still be home." She looked up at him and smiled gently. "I'm sorry if I've disrupted your life."

"It isn't the disruption that's hard to deal with," he said. "It's the damnable frustration I feel whenever I'm around you. And you foster that, you know. You like it, I think."

Confirming his observation, she smiled. "Frustrated how?"

"Just looking at you makes me want to tear your clothes off. You're sexy as hell, and you know it. What I want to know is why you can flaunt it like you do but you can't face it when it comes right down to it."

"I can face it," she said.

She sat still, mesmerized, as he got up and came to stoop in front of her. Taking her hand, he brought it to his mouth and pressed a kiss on her palm. His eyes met hers, daring her to pull away, daring her to stop him.

"As crazy as you make me, Cindy, this is the most excitement I have had in years," he whispered. "You thrill me."

Slowly, she felt that control she had been gripping so tightly slipping through her fingers. Countering that feeling and trying to get that control back, she said, "You're a good-looking man, Dusty. I can see why Red wanted you."

He smiled. "Can you? I would think you'd find it baffling."

"Why?" she asked. "Just because I wouldn't jump into bed with you last night?"

"That's part of it," he said, stroking his hand down her arm. "Your eyes say yes, your body says yes, but then you open your mouth and *no* comes out."

"Is that why you got a date for tonight? To find someone who'd say yes?"

He didn't like the way that made him sound, and he straightened slightly. "No. How do you know that I didn't have the date planned for days?"

"Did you?"

He looked at her honestly and finally said, "No. I asked her last night when I got home."

"Last night?" She couldn't fight the feeling of betrayal that washed over her, and pushing him back, she got up and ambled across the room. "Well. Good thing I *didn't* sleep with you. It would have proved my point."

"What point?"

"The one about too much being at stake. Speaking purely emotionally, of course."

He stood up and set his hands on his hips. "Hey, if you had slept with me last night, I wouldn't have been going anywhere tonight."

"So it was payback? Blackmail? The if-you-don't-sleep-with-me-I'll-find-someone-who-will kind of thing?"

He shook his head. "No, that's not it. It's more like the I've-got-to-get-Cindy-Hartzell-out-of-my-head-before-I-go-insane kind of thing."

"And did it work?"

"Frankly, no. I'm here, aren't I?"

"You don't have to be. In fact, Red's probably sitting up waiting for you."

She started across the room to the refrigerator but he caught her arm and flung her around. "If you want to know the truth, Cindy, I'd rather be here yelling at you, steeped in the deepest frustration I have ever known in my life, than to be in bed with her! Can you understand that?"

She looked at him, stunned for a moment. "Why?"

"Because," he said, pulling her against him, his arms brooking no debate, "you are the most exciting, most beautiful, most maddening woman that I've ever met in my life and I can't stop thinking that your lovemaking is probably as reckless and passionate as everything else you do.'' He kissed her hard, bringing her to her toes as his tongue probed deep inside her mouth and his hands slid down her back, crushing her hips against him. ''Is it, Cindy?'' he whispered. ''Are you as passionate as you seem?''

She tried to control her breathing, but it came as heavy as his. ''Are you?''

He trembled as his hands slipped under her shirt. ''You're about to find out,'' he said.

She could have objected, could have stopped him, could have allowed her reasoning and her rules to kick in. But Cindy had never been that good with rules, and she couldn't remember any of the reasons anymore.

Something about betrayal, she thought. Something about emotion. Something about getting close, getting hurt. Risking everything.

But right now, all that mattered was that reckless desire pulsing through her and his hands touching her in places that made her shiver.

She moaned and slid her arms around him, and he lifted her in his arms and carried her to the bed. Just before he set her down, he kissed her, hard, and with the greatest intent she had ever experienced, and he whispered, ''Tell me to go, Cindy. This is your last chance.''

Her answer was to reach for him, grab the opening in his shirt and tear it open, sending buttons popping off and rolling on the hard floor. Trembling, she grabbed his belt, unbuckling it.

As if a fire had been set and then doused with fuel, they tore at each other's clothes until they lay in a heap on the floor, until their passion was unhindered, until there was nothing between them except a delirium that reached a peak and hovered there for an eternity.

They made fierce, unbridled, unbearable love, until they were both glistening and exhausted, until neither could speak, until neither could let go.

Then, wearier from the lovemaking than she had been from the grueling hours fighting g-forces in her plane, Cindy fell into a deep sleep, wrapped in his arms. The rightness of it intruded on her dreams, reminding her of what a unique fit his arms seemed to be. Hinting that it was a place where she belonged as she had never belonged before.

CINDY WOKE WITH A START as the first colors of dawn shone through the window and painted her walls.

Dusty hadn't left her side. He was still here, still holding her. But that couldn't be, she told herself. Soon enough, he'd awaken and she'd see that look in his eyes, the one that asked how the hell he'd wound up here last night and how he could leave now without seeming like a jerk. Then, getting up and trying to make idle conversation while he dressed, he'd probably call her by some other name, decline her offer for breakfast, then say that he needed to get flying before the wind picked up. For the rest of the day, they'd act awkward around each other and he wouldn't be able to wait to get home and forget any of it ever happened.

That was the way the game was played. That was why she rarely played it anymore.

But she had played it last night, and she would be damned before she'd sit still and let herself be the loser this time.

Quietly, she got up, showered, pulled on a pair of cutoffs and a T-shirt and left the apartment. By the time he woke, she thought, she would be the one pretending it hadn't mattered.

Chapter Ten

Dusty woke to an empty bed, and he sat up and looked around the small apartment. There was no sign of Cindy.

Outside, he heard the sound of the plane's engine, and he got out of bed and went to the front door. When he opened it, he saw through the hangar doors that Cindy was about to take off.

Frowning, he turned back to the bed, where all that passion had erupted last night. If he'd been dreaming, he wouldn't be standing here naked in her apartment, he told himself. It had happened, in spite of her fears of his making light of it, in spite of her terror that she'd grow attached.

But instead of his being flip and acting as if it hadn't meant a thing, *she* was doing it.

He jerked on his pants and found his shirt still lying on the floor, and as he tugged it on, he told himself this was her way. Do unto others before they can do unto you. Counter vulnerability with aggression.

He slammed the door to her apartment as he left, then got into his truck and drove home before she could notice he was gone. By the time he had showered and come back, she was on her second load of the morning, and they still hadn't exchanged a word.

He got out of the truck and heard the plane circling overhead, and suddenly her voice came across the radio. "Morning, Dusty."

Frowning, he picked up the mike and looked at her plane in the sky. If she was speaking to him, in even a remotely friendly way, it sort of threw off his theory. Maybe he was wrong, he thought.

"Morning," he said. "You okay?"

"Great," she said. "Look at that sunrise."

He squinted at the sun just rising over the trees. "Yeah. You sure got an early start."

She was quiet for a moment. "Lot to do. No use in waiting."

"Oh, I could think of a few uses for waiting."

Again, silence.

"Cindy? Can you hear me?"

Her radio hummed for a moment before she answered. "You'd better get flying, Dusty. We'll never get finished today if you don't."

The fact that she would pull rank, after a night of such intimacy, made him angry, and his face reddened. Why was she doing this? "I intend to, Cindy. Don't start that stuff with me. Over."

"What stuff?" she asked, irritated.

"I get the message, okay? Never you fear." He slapped the mike back on its hook and headed for his plane.

"Dusty?" He heard her calling him, but, ignoring her, he set about getting the plane out of the hangar.

DUSTY COULDN'T REMEMBER working this hard since 1989, when it had rained so much that the farmers hadn't been able to get their high-boys in the fields to spray and had had no recourse but to hire crop dusters for every bit of spraying they did. This year there wasn't rain to blame, though, but Cindy's coercion in getting all the farmers to jump Sid's ship and return to Dusty's.

Part of him was angry at how easy it had been for her. This much work could have turned his business around completely. He wouldn't have had to sell out. It would all still be his, and he wouldn't have ever had to meet Cindy Hartzell or have his ego stomped out like a cigarette butt and he wouldn't have spent so much time trying not to think about how wonderful and volatile her lovemaking with him had been.

And it wouldn't have made him so crazy when she seemed so preoccupied with flying that she barely had time to utter a passing comment.

Still, he couldn't deny the fact that he wouldn't wish her away for anything. He'd hate to think of her not being there, in her outrageous little T-shirts and cut-offs, every morning. His father had once told him that men "just felt good" when they were around beautiful women. They laughed more and strutted and had more energy than ever before. He supposed now that his father was right. Seeing her, even if she ignored him completely, always lifted his spirits. But then, like a wind in the wake of a tornado, his attitude got mixed up, ignited and became filled with a million other attitudes and emotions that tainted his good mood.

It was the damnedest thing.

Even so, he couldn't wait to get to work each morning, and he dreaded the moment he had to go home each night.

CINDY GAVE DUSTY the day off that Sunday, since they had caught up on all the work that couldn't wait until Monday. She wanted to go to church, she said. She felt it was time.

What she didn't tell him was that she hadn't darkened the doors of a Baptist church since she'd left Yazoo City. Oh, she had worshiped at the Vatican when she was in Rome, even though she wasn't Catholic. She had prayed in a Greek cathedral in Athens and a mosque in Saudi Arabia. But nothing compared to the little Southern Baptist church where she had been raised, right in the buckle of the Bible Belt.

As she dressed for church in a modest dress with a Victorian neckline and a full skirt, and pulled her hair up in a French twist, she told herself that it would be good to go back. When she'd left, she had hated everything that church had stood for. She'd hated the piety that demanded purity from everyone, but conveniently forgot the sin involved in gossip and snooping. She'd hated the committees that made it their business to straighten out their members and their members' children. She'd hated the self-righteous good works that made less fortunate people feel even less fortunate.

But that was before she had understood any of it. She'd spent years now, thinking about what made that church tick, what made it such a vital force in the community and why she missed it so much. It had just been in the last few months that it occurred to her why.

Despite the fact that the church was filled with sinful people who couldn't see their own sins but had a keen sight where others' sins were concerned, the church was a pure institution that set standards for loving and caring and nurturing the community. Standards that many of its members would never have come close to reaching alone. It was the church that brought them together on Sundays and Wednesdays, the church that made children try to walk straight lines for fear that another church member might see them messing up, the church that forgave and forgave and forgave, even if the people within it couldn't.

It was that community offered by her church, that belonging, that forgiveness that she sought now. She would have a home there, even if she didn't have one with her family, she thought. The church would not turn her away.

She felt a flutter of nervous anticipation as she pulled into the gravel parking lot and got out of her car. Several congregation members on their way turned and waved at her, smiling as if they'd been waiting for her. Straightening to her full height, which still wasn't that tall even in her heels, she held her chin high, smiled as if she knew she belonged here, and walked through the doors.

Her family was sitting in their usual section, with her parents in the middle row of the sanctuary and her brothers behind them, each with a whole pew for their respective families. Taking a deep breath, she walked up the center aisle, stopped at her parents' pew and slipped in next to them as if she'd been invited.

"Hi, Mom, Dad," she said.

Her mother gaped at her. "Well . . . I didn't expect you to show up here. I didn't think you went to church anymore."

Cindy smiled. "Is it okay if I sit here? I could move if you're embarrassed."

Her mother compressed her lips and sent an eloquent look to her father. "No, that's quite all right. You're welcome to sit with us."

"Great." She turned around and spoke to her nephews behind her, waved at the nieces behind them, and then to her brothers and their wives.

Then she glanced around at the familiar faces of the congregation, all of whom seemed trained on her, as if waiting for her to do something completely outrageous. For a moment, her mind flipped through possibilities. She could volunteer to sing a solo after the minister welcomed the visitors, she thought. Something by David Bowie. "Rock 'n' Roll Suicide," perhaps.

Or . . . she could frighten them all and pretend to speak in tongues. Nothing threw a Baptist worse than speaking in tongues, she mused. They liked their services nice and neat, quiet, civilized.

As she turned over the various possibilities, she glanced toward the doors and saw Dusty dressed in a black suit with a white shirt and tie that accented the tan on his face. He looked like one of the tycoons on "Knots Landing," she thought, complete with gold cuff links and a killer smile.

She started to wave, but then spotted the redhead behind him, and the little girl trailing behind her.

She saw Dusty look up and see her, and she quickly turned back around and faced the front.

Still, she felt people watching her, felt that redhead watching her, felt *Dusty* watching her. They expected a surprise from her, some sort of entertainment to tell all their friends about, some sort of show that would upstage the pastor.

So she gave them something that surprised them all, something none of them expected. As the service began, she sat perfectly still, with a serene smile on her face, and she listened to every word the pastor had to say, took part in every hymn the congregation had to sing and prayed with all the fervor she'd ever felt each time she bowed her head.

In short, she worshiped, as deeply and as purely as she could.

And when the service was over, she could see that her plan had worked. As disappointed as everyone had been, they were all surprised.

Her mother seemed pleased as she followed her out of the pew. "Thank you, Cindy. You behaved quite well."

Cindy smiled. "I am over thirty, Mama. I do know how to conduct myself."

"Of course you know," her father interjected. "We taught you right. Doesn't mean you've ever chosen to follow it. Have you decided to accept my offer yet?"

"Actually, no," she said. "It's doing very well. We've been busier than I ever imagined."

"Well, there's going to be some bad weather this week. I hope you won't try to fly in all that."

"Of course not," she said. "When the crops are wet, they dilute the chemicals. We have to wait until they dry out. Besides, we can't fly in the clouds with no navigational equipment. It's impossible to tell which end is up."

"Much like flying at night," Hyram quipped. "I guess I can rest easier knowing you won't be playing the Red Baron for a few days." He paused and glanced back at their family waiting to thread into the congested aisle. "I suppose you expect an invitation for lunch?"

Cindy, who had hoped for such an invitation, felt as if she'd been clubbed and her expression collapsed. "Actually, no, Daddy. I have plans."

"What plans?" her mother asked. "What's more important than Sunday dinner with your family?"

The contradictions maddened her, but she didn't wilt. "I wasn't invited, remember?"

"Of course you're invited," her mother said. "How would it look if you were here and we didn't invite you?"

"Like you didn't want me there?" she asked, blinking back the tears rimming her eyes.

"Cindy, there you go, looking for something to pin on us," her father said. "No one said we didn't want you there. If you want to eat lunch with us, you're welcome to."

"That's okay," Cindy said. "I really do have plans. Maybe next Sunday."

Cindy glanced across the crowd of people leaving the church and saw Dusty following his redhead out. The woman was pretty, in a simple sort of way, and there were no long nails or black roots to rile Dusty about. But the proprietary way she clung to his arm made Cindy angry. Whether that anger was directed at the woman, Dusty or herself, she wasn't sure.

Deciding not to let him walk out without introducing her, she pushed through the crowd and made her way to Dusty.

"I didn't know you went to church," she said.

He looked back at her over his shoulder. "Sometimes. When I don't have to work. I've been told I need it."

"I'll second that," she said, her eyes dancing with that effervescent mischief that made him woefully uncomfortable. He was afraid she'd say something embarrassing to his little girlfriend, she thought. He was afraid she'd stand right here, in the middle of

Calvary Baptist Church, and tell her that they had slept together last week.

"Uh...Bev," he said, reluctantly. "I'd like you to meet Cindy Hartzell. My..."

He got hung up on the word *boss* so she helped him out by offering, "Svengali."

Bev looked a little confused, so dismissing it, Cindy took her hand. "Hi. It's great meeting you."

"I...I've heard a lot about you," Bev said.

"Have you now?" Cindy asked, moving her amused gaze back to Dusty. "Well, it's probably all true, and then some."

She spoke to the child, then raised up and patted Dusty's cheek. "Nice little potential family," she whispered as she passed.

He didn't answer as she made her way to the front door, where the pastor greeted people as they left to go home. She waited for her turn, then took his hand, knowing that Dusty and Bev were behind her. "Brother Allen, it was so good to hear you preach again. I felt like you were talking just to me. You weren't, were you?"

"No, I wasn't," he chuckled, patting her hand. "It's good to have you back in the flock, Cindy. You always brought a little life to our congregation."

"Some people don't like to have life in the congregation," she said. "But I'm back whether they like it or not. Listen, Brother Allen, I would love it if you and Mrs. Allen would join me for lunch. My treat."

The man threw his head back and laughed. "Well, now, Cindy, I don't think I could think of a more pleasant way to spend the afternoon."

"Great," she said. "Why don't we meet at Penn's?"

"Give me twenty minutes," he said. "We'll look forward to it."

Feeling as if she'd just made a giant stride in being accepted again, Cindy walked with a light step out to her car. As she got in, she noted Dusty and Bev separating, the woman getting into her own car as he headed for his. He backed out before she did, and when he reached the edge of the parking lot, he went a different direction from the one Bev had taken.

Cindy smiled. Maybe he wasn't as enamored with the woman as she'd thought. Or maybe he was mad at her for being so flip about the whole thing. Or maybe he was going to go home to change and spend the afternoon with Bev, and not give Cindy another thought.

Pushing the thought out of her mind, Cindy headed for the restaurant and decided that today was going to be wonderful no matter what happened.

IT WAS RAINING by the time Cindy and the reverend and his wife left the restaurant, laughing and reminiscing about things that Cindy had done as a child…but even more about some of the things she'd done as an adult.

There was no condemnation there, she thought warmly as they got into their car and drove away. Only acceptance and love. She only wished more of Brother Allen's congregation—her family included—could understand that concept.

Dusty's truck was at the hangar when she pulled up, and an inexplicable feeling of satisfaction—and indeed, relief—washed over her. He wasn't with Bev. He was here ... waiting for her.

She went in and found him up on the wing of his plane, waxing the finish.

"What are you doing?" she asked.

He glanced down at her and she could see that he was irritated with her about something. "What does it look like?"

"It looks like you're waxing the plane. But why today?"

"Because on weekdays we're flying them," he said. "And they need it. They didn't stay this clean by themselves, you know."

"I know." She sighed. "I just thought you might have better things to do. Like spending the afternoon with your girlfriend and her daughter."

"Look, she's just a friend, okay? I've been out with her, but there's no burning romance there."

"You don't owe me an explanation."

"I know I don't. But just in case you thought—"

"I didn't think anything," she said. "Nothing at all."

"All right then." He rubbed harder, wiping the white filmy wax off the yellow paint. "So you ate with the preacher, did you?"

"Yes," she said. "He's an old friend."

"Did your family cut you out again?"

Her cheeks stung and her smile faded. "No. Why?"

"Because everybody knows that the Hartzells always eat Sunday dinner together. They practically fill up the steak house."

Cindy started toward the stairs. "I'm gonna go change."

"Then they did dump on you, didn't they? Even though you went to church and everything."

"I didn't go to church for them, okay? I went for me."

"To prove something?"

"No," she shouted. "To worship. What a concept, huh? That somebody could see church not as a social gathering but as a place of worship. I happen to believe in what they teach there, Dusty, even though ninety-five percent of the rest of the congregation couldn't grasp it if they confronted the burning bush themselves!" Furious, she started up the stairs, but before she reached her door, she flung around. "Why are you doing this?"

"Why are *you?*" he returned. "You're the one who's had a chip on your shoulder since last weekend. You're the one who's been walking around here avoiding me like the plague."

"I have not! We've been busy. I've been working!"

"Have you once mentioned what happened between us? Have you even acknowledged it?"

"Have you?" she volleyed.

"I tried," he said. "But then you got haughty and started pulling rank, reminding me where my place in this outfit is."

"That's your interpretation, not mine! I'm just taking care of business. If you can't take a one-night stand, then you probably ought to give them up."

With that, she slammed into her apartment, leaving him on the wing of his plane, staring, astounded.

In seconds, he had leapt down and was bolting up her stairs. "Open up, Cindy! Now!"

She didn't answer, so he threw the door open himself and stormed in. He saw her in the doorway of the kitchen, with her hands planted on her hips.

"First of all, what happened between us was not a one-night stand. Not until you made it that! Second of all, you're the one who popped out of bed and took off into the wild blue yonder even before I had cracked my eyes open. And third, you're the one who has made it this big taboo subject for the last week, like we'll both self-destruct if we acknowledge that we enjoyed it!"

She raised her hands, shaking her head. "Look, I'm not in the mood for this. Just let me change clothes and I'll wax the other plane."

"No!" he shouted. "You may be my boss where those airplanes are concerned, but on off hours, we're equals, and I want to know—no, I *demand* to know—what the hell is your problem?"

"It shouldn't have happened, okay?" she shouted. "It always messes everything up! It just shouldn't have!"

"It won't mess things up if you don't let it, Cindy," he said, his voice dropping to a softer pitch as he strode closer to her. "The truth is it was the best sex I've ever had and I liked holding you and sleeping next to you. And I would have loved waking up with you, if I'd had the chance."

"Why?" she asked. "When you have Bev? Do you want to alternate back and forth between us? Choose her when you need stability and me when you need excitement?"

"I don't do that," he said. "And half the time I don't know whether that excitement you're always throwing up to me is an act or part of your real character. It's like you think people expect you to be unpredictable. Why are you always giving them what they want?" He walked over to her suitcase, still packed and lying on the floor. "And this... Why don't you unpack this damn thing? Act like somebody who's going to stay awhile. Or aren't you sure that you are, yet? Is that why you don't want to get involved with me? Because you're afraid you might have to unpack and put down a root or two?"

"I have roots!" she shouted. "And what I live out of is none of your business!"

"Then why are you so afraid of me?" he shouted. "Why?"

"Because!" Tears rolled down her face as she clutched at her head. "Because I'm trying to do something here. I'm trying to do it alone. I'm trying to do it without getting hurt and feeling the need to run away. I don't want to have to run away this time, Dusty.''

He took her shoulders, made her look up at him. "Trust me, Cindy. I'm not going to drive you away. Your parents might, but I won't."

She fell against him, and he held her as she cried, awed by the degree of passion in those tears, the intensity of pain in her sobs.

Then, just as quickly as they had come, those tears disappeared and she looked up at him, wiping her eyes. "Thank you, Dusty. I'm okay now."

"Are you sure?" he asked softly.

She managed a smile. "Yeah. Must be that time of the month."

"Why is it that men can't get away with suggesting that, but if a woman says it to discount any real emotions she's feeling, it's okay?"

"I'm not discounting anything." She took a deep breath and looked up at him. "You're not going to let me get away with much, are you?"

"No, darlin'. I'm not."

She turned back to the kitchen counter and poured a cup of coffee. "Well, just the same, we're not going to sleep together again."

"Fine," he said, "if that's the way you want it."

"It is." She stirred a spoonful of sugar into her coffee, and he noted the defensive way she held herself, the guard she was putting up even now. He would have to be satisfied with the brief glimpse of her vulnerability, he thought, but somehow it was enough.

For now.

He went up behind her, grazed his lips across her neck and felt her shiver in response. "I'll be waxing the plane," he said. "See you when you come down."

Cindy turned around and watched him leave her apartment without another word.

Chapter Eleven

"If this rain doesn't stop, I'm going to lose my mind." A bolt of lightning flashed in the distance, and Cindy took a step back from the open hangar door and bumped into Dusty. Quickly, she moved away from him, muttering, "Sorry."

He let the apology go, but didn't take his eyes from her. "Is it really the rain, or being in such close quarters with me for four days in a row?"

She tossed him a look, but didn't know how to answer the question. She had always loved rain before, and she'd been fascinated by the cinematic spectacle of a lightning storm, but enough was enough. Especially when it kept them grounded as the work piled up. But it wasn't even that that bothered her so much now. It was Dusty.

He'd hung around here from daylight until dark every day this week, claiming that he wanted to be here in case the clouds suddenly parted and allowed him the chance to get something done. But he knew as well as she that the farmers didn't want their wet crops sprayed. It would take at least several hours of hot sun to dry the plants out before they could spray them. For all practical purposes, Dusty could have stayed home.

But he'd been here, breathing down her neck, following her with a gaze that suggested that he was the one in control, that, if he got it into his head, he could make her melt into a little puddle.

But he didn't push it. He didn't try. And she couldn't help admitting that she walked the line between relief and disappointment.

The sky grew darker as the storm progressed, and in the distance, she saw three jagged bolts lighting up the sky, then casting it into darkness again. "You might as well go home, Dusty," she said. "There's no need to stay."

"What about you?" he asked. "All that thunder and lightning...it gets pretty frightening sometimes."

She grinned at the notion that she might be afraid. "Hey, I once swam across San Francisco Bay in a lightning storm. It doesn't scare me."

He offered a laugh that said he didn't believe a word, and she matched his grin. "Yeah, you're a real tough kid, aren't you?"

She shrugged. "I'm not afraid of a stupid little storm."

"Then how come you unplugged everything in the hangar?"

"I didn't want to have to replace it if lightning struck," she said. "Caution and fear are not the same things. The weather report says the worst part of the storm is in Vicksburg and will be here in a few hours. By the time it gets here I'll be all tucked in and sleeping right through it.''

"All right," he said, pulling his keys from his pocket. "I guess I'll go, then."

"I'll lock up," she said. "Be careful going home."

She watched as he ambled out to his truck, not at all daunted by the sharp beat of the rain on his shoulders. As he reached his car door, the sky lit up again, casting him in silhouette for a second. He was beautiful, she thought, in the best ways, but she'd fallen for beautiful men before.

She felt that old tension creeping up inside her again, the same tension she always felt when feelings she couldn't control began to try to control her. She was right to feel it, she thought, for if she'd heeded that tension while dating her husband, she would have realized she was nothing more than bait, a maddening challenge for him. As long as she refused to sleep with him, he had showered her with gifts and flowers and affection like she'd never known before. He had even married her.

She watched as Dusty started his truck and pulled onto the main road, slowly disappearing from her sight. Unbidden, the memory of her stupidity and blindness filled her heart. Love was such a damaging thing; it attacked in places where people were most innocent. And it had attacked her with Anthony, promising her that nothing would ever make her feel lonely or inadequate again.

But it was short-lived. Three days after their wedding, three days after the first time he conquered her, she had caught him in bed with her "friend."

Inadequate didn't begin to describe what she had felt after that. She could play a good game, she thought, and she could flirt and tease and turn heads with the best of them. But she could never allow that emotion to waylay her again.

The lightning seemed to be walking closer, with jagged legs that reached miles, and she began to slide the doors to the hangar shut. But the emotions threatening to ambush her, along with a desire that had only grown with the one intimate experience she'd had with Dusty, couldn't be shut out so easily.

THE SOUND OF SOMEONE banging on her door woke Cindy in the middle of the night, and, not bothering to pull a robe over her nightshirt, she jumped out of bed and grabbed the jeans hanging over a chair. As she ran, clutching the jeans in her hand, she realized it had to be Dusty. No one else could have gotten through the hangar.

The banging grew more intense as she reached the door, and, breathless, she swung it open. "Dusty, it's 3:00 a.m! What is it?"

"Tornadoes," he said, grabbing her hand and pulling her out the door.

She stumbled down the stairs after him, struggling to orient herself. "What?"

"Tornadoes," he repeated. "Several have touched down already in Jackson, and one hit Benton a few minutes ago. The whole county is under tornado warning."

They reached the concrete floor of the hangar, and she shivered at the cold beneath her bare feet. "Where are we going, for heaven's sake?"

"To the post office," he said. "It's a federal disaster shelter with a basement and it's closer than my house."

"But my shoes!" she shouted as he tried to pull her out into the rain. "I haven't even got my pants on!"

"I've got some boots and you can put the pants on in the car." He opened the passenger door to his truck and shoved her in.

"Why can't we just stay here?" she asked when he'd gotten in on his side and was cranking the engine and pulling out into the road.

"That building is worse than a house trailer in a tornado. It's nothing but prefabricated aluminum."

"But the tornado probably would have missed us." She struggled to pull her jeans over her wet legs. "I'd have been willing to take my chances. This is a lousy way to wake up."

"Excuse me for bothering with you," he said over the sound of the storm. "I have a basement at home. I could have stayed but I was worried about you. I tried calling you, but you must not have heard the phone ringing. You know, you really ought to get an extension put in the apartment."

"So people like you can wake me up in the middle of the night to give weather reports? No, thanks."

Immediately, she regretted her words, and from his expression, she feared he might pull over and let her out on the side of the road. "For your information, Miss Swam-across-San-Francisco-Bay-in-a-lightning-storm, we had a series of tornadoes in '92 that destroyed almost an entire community. A friend of mine was killed when the tornado rammed through his house."

She ducked her head, then brought her eyes back to his. "I'm sorry, Dusty. I'm just cranky when I wake up. You didn't have to go to all this trouble. I would have been all right."

"How, when you were sound asleep?"

"Well, how did you know about it?"

"I'm closer to the town. There were warning sirens, and then I listened to the radio. But out here you don't know it's on you until it gets here."

He turned a corner, sending the tires skidding around on the wet pavement as they reached the street where the post office was.

Cindy zipped her jeans, snapped them, then tried to take a deep breath. "Oh, look, Dusty. It's stopped raining. Why don't you just take me back home—"

"Holy Mary," Dusty said. "It's always calm before a tornado." He punched the accelerator to the ground and flew toward the post-office parking lot, where several other cars were parked.

The sky lit up with lightning, three flashes in a row as they got out, and in the distance, Dusty saw the narrow outline of a twister that was still several miles away. "Get in there!" he shouted. "Down in the basement. Hurry!"

Cindy looked in the direction he'd been looking, and as the sky lit up again, she saw the tornado making its way toward them. "It's coming!" she shouted.

But before they could reach the door, another car headed up the road toward them. "Oh, no. It's the Prentisses," Dusty said. "They've got two sets of twins, a two-month-old baby and Al's eighty-five-year-old grandmother. They'll never make it inside!"

He opened the door and tried to shove her in. "Go on in. I'm going to help them."

The sky lit up again as the car pulled to the curb out front, and Cindy saw that the tornado had come threateningly closer in just the few moments since she first saw it. In only a few minutes more, it would be upon them. "Dusty, there's no time!"

He lit out toward the car before she could stop him, and she watched as he helped the mother out. She was clutching the tiny baby to her chest. He grabbed a pair of toddler twins, handed them to their father, helped the grandmother to the sidewalk, then went after the three-year-olds crying in the back of the station wagon, refusing to come out.

Cindy held the door open as Al Prentiss rushed in with his babies, and she heard the distant roar of the tornado as it came closer with every second. She saw the struggle Dusty was having with one of the three-year-olds at the same time as he was trying to help the grandmother toward the building, and she opened the door to shout for him to hurry. The wind knocked the door out of her hands and threw it back against the bricks, and she fell down, grabbing the wall to get back up.

Al Prentiss was just coming back up the steps, when Dusty bolted in with two three-year-olds screaming at the top of their lungs and the grandmother huffing with the effort of walking faster than she'd walked in years.

They had only started down the steps to the basement when the freight-train sound of the tornado engulfed them, and the force of breaking glass and debris flying against the building shook them.

In the basement, two dozen or so people crouched in frozen silence as the building above them endured the havoc the tornado wreaked.

And then, within thirty seconds, it was gone.

Even the Prentiss twins were silent in the aftermath of the tornado. Finally, Dusty stood up. "Everybody stay here," he said. "I'll go see what the damage is."

Cindy leaned back against the wall and hugged her knees as she watched Dusty climb the steps. The sudden gravity of what had happened clutched at her, and as she looked around, she saw the fear on everyone else's face.

In minutes, Dusty came back down.

"How is it, Dusty?" one of the men asked.

"Uh…" Cindy could see on his face the struggle to divert a panic since the news he had for them would surely cause one. "It could be worse."

"Aw, hell," one of the other men said, getting to his feet. "We're gonna have to see for ourselves sooner or later."

"Careful," Dusty said. "There's broken glass everywhere, and there's a big hole knocked in one of the outside walls." He turned around and scanned the expectant faces packed into the small basement. His gaze landed on one of the men. "Stew, you might want to go on across the street. Looks like your gas station was pretty damaged."

"Aw, no." Stew Hancock and his wife got up and started slowly up the stairs.

"Some of the cars had windows knocked out," Dusty said. "My truck is one of them. And up and down the street, well, it's hard to tell. . . ."

Slowly, one by one, the victims made their way out of the shelter, embarking on a world that had been altered in a matter of seconds.

The rain was just beginning to fall again as they spilled out into the night, and the air seemed charged with a force that Cindy hadn't known before. As she looked around her, experiencing the horror of the things the town had lost, while the others marveled at the buildings left untouched, avoiding power lines and stepping over debris that had flown for miles in the ravaging winds, she suddenly realized that it had taken a disaster to give her what she'd come home for.

Suddenly she belonged, and she realized that this town, and these losses, were as much hers as theirs.

Still awkward in Dusty's boots and her nightshirt and jeans, she helped some of the men clear the street in front of the post office so they could each go home to face their own personal disasters, and then she went back to Dusty's truck and cleaned the glass off of the seats.

"You ready to go see if you still have a business?" he asked softly behind her.

She turned around. "Oh, no. I hadn't thought of that. You don't think the planes . . . ?"

He got in and cranked the engine, which magically purred to life as if nothing horrible had occurred. "I hope not," he whispered.

They drove quietly through the town, now and then stopping to remove some piece of debris from the street or detouring because of a fallen tree in the road. Some of the land beyond the roads seemed untouched, but elsewhere, acres of timber seemed destroyed.

Cindy hugged her arms around herself and tried to stop shivering.

"Cold?" he asked.

She shook her head. "No, but . . . I can't stop shaking."

"I know," he said. Reaching over, he took her hand.

They held their breath as they turned up the road where the hangar was, and Cindy looked over at him. "Dusty, don't you want to check your house?"

"I will after we check the hangar. I just need to make sure the planes are all right."

She let his words sink in as they made their way up the long stretch of road. That he cared more about planes that weren't even his than he did about his house surprised her. But it was no more surprising than the way he'd ventured out into the storm for her, when he could have been safe in his own basement.

"Ready?" he asked as they came to the turnoff to the hangar.

"As ready as I'll ever be," she said.

They held their breath as he turned and immediately they saw that the roof of the shed that housed the holding tanks was lying on the ground. One of the tanks had been blown over and the old riding lawn mower they kept parked outside had been blown a hundred yards into the field next door.

But the hangar was still standing. Not even a window had been blown out.

"Oh, thank God," Cindy said, wilting back against the seat.

They went inside, just to confirm that the planes hadn't been damaged. From the looks of things, the tornado hadn't come through that way. The damage outside was from the wind created by the storm.

When they were satisfied that everything was intact, they got back in and drove to Dusty's. Along the way, the houses seemed to be still standing, indicating that the tornado hadn't ripped through here, either.

Dusty's house was untouched. The moment he saw it, he began to laugh—a long, hearty, relieved laugh—and Cindy reached over to hug him. "It's okay. Everything is okay."

They went into the dark house and were instantly greeted by Moon-baby and Dog, whom he had let inside before he'd left. The electricity had been knocked out, and the house was cold. "I have a gas stove," he said. "I'll make us some instant coffee."

"That'll be great," Cindy said, lowering onto his couch. "I wonder how my parents are."

He picked up the phone and held it to his ear. "Phones are out. But they're probably fine. The Hartzell houses are built like fortresses."

"Yeah," she whispered. "I guess so."

He made the coffee and brought in two mugs. Cindy took hers, sipped, then looked at him in the darkness as he sat down next to her. "You were really something, you know. The way you helped the Prentisses."

"Well, what was I gonna do? Just let them get blown away?"

"You almost got blown away yourself. Dusty, why didn't you just stay here? Why did you come to get me?"

"I told you why." He leaned his head back on the couch.

"But why were you worried?"

He looked at her then, and a slow smile traveled across his face. "Because if you'd gotten blown away, I might never have the chance to get you in the sack again."

For a moment she just looked at him, and then she started to laugh. He laughed, too, and she fell against him, more comfortable with their intimacy in laughter than she had been since the night they'd slept together.

If he asked tonight, she wondered, would she allow it to happen again? And even as she asked herself, she knew the answer was yes.

But he didn't ask. Instead, he took her mug from her when she had finished and got to his feet. "Come on. I'll take you home. You have lights, so it's warmer there."

Confused, she stood up, still barefoot and still wearing her nightshirt and jeans, and faced him with a countenance she knew was too vulnerable for her own good.

He reached over, slid his fingers into her hair and pulled her into a soft, sweet kiss that ignited desire all the way through her bloodstream. And then he let her go, taking her hand and pulling her through the dark house.

She didn't say a word as they got into the truck, and as they drove back to the hangar, she realized that she had laid out the rules. He was just following them. All she had to do was change them, and she could be with him through the night.

But something inside her prevented her from doing it.

Fear, she told herself, even stronger than the fear that she'd felt tonight. Fear of intimacy, fear of giving, fear of having it all thrown back in her face. She was bright enough to know it for what it was, but for the life of her, she didn't know a way around it.

When they got to the hangar, he unlocked the door for her and let her in. She turned back to him as he lingered at the door. "Aren't you coming in?"

"No, I should get some sleep," he said. "I'll be back in the morning. I might sleep until seven or so today."

They looked at each other for an eloquent moment, and finally she touched his shoulder. "Thanks, Dusty."

"Don't mention it." He leaned forward to kiss her cheek, then took a step back. "See you later. Try to get some sleep."

He closed the door behind him, and she leaned against it, trying to decide what to do with these raging feelings she hadn't expected when she'd gone to bed last night.

But they were there, and there was nothing she could do about them. Somehow, she would learn to deal with them.

THE NEXT MORNING, Dusty arrived as the news report was just coming across the radio. Hundreds of people had been left homeless in last night's storm, and as Cindy heard about their plight on the radio, Dusty saw the tears in her eyes.

"We were lucky, weren't we?"

"Yeah," she said. "There must be something we can do."

He shrugged. "I thought I'd ride around this morning until I found people who needed help cleaning up. Then I might get some old clothes together to take down to the church for anyone who needs them. Maybe give some money. Someone must know what they need."

"Toothbrushes," she said, imagining the houses that had been completely wiped out, all the way down to the plumbing, leaving nothing at all behind. "They'll need toothbrushes, and sheets, and towels, and blankets..."

Dusty looked up at her. It was almost as if she had some intimate association with these people. "Yeah, I guess so."

"Imagine waking up one day and having everything you own blown to kingdom come," she whispered. "Everything. Makes me glad I don't have anything."

He sighed. "Look, if you want we can go right over to the church and see if there's anything they need."

"I know something they need," she said. "They'll need a place to house these people for a night or two until they can find them places. We could let them stay here."

Dusty frowned. "Here? In the hangar?"

"Sure," she said. "We could move the planes out just for the night and set up some cots. Have someone bring food in. Maybe a live band." Her eyes were growing more animated with every moment.

"A live band?"

"Well, yeah. To get their minds off their troubles. We could make a party out of it."

"I doubt if any of these people feel like a party," he said. "And I don't like the idea of those planes being left out all night. Anything could happen. They'd be too accessible."

"Not if we had the hangar doors open. Then we'd be able to watch the planes all night."

He stood up and gaped at her. "You're serious about this, aren't you?"

Her smile was the brightest he'd seen all week. "Yes, I am."

Something inside him groaned, but not wanting to seem like a heel, he threw up his hands. "Why do I have the feeling that you can't be talked out of this?"

Grinning ear to ear, Cindy grabbed her bag and followed him out to his truck to go offer the hangar to the church.

NO ONE WOULD HAVE GUESSED that the reason for the gathering at Webb's Flying Service that evening was to shelter people who'd lost their homes. From the looks of things, it was the best party of the decade.

A live band from Jackson played rock music on the tarmac, while tornado victims danced and ate to their hearts' content from the food provided by most of the restaurants in town. Some of the congregation of the Calvary Baptist Church showed up with truckloads of clothing and other items, and tried to look undaunted at the goings-on there that night.

When her parents showed up to find her brothers partying down with the rest of them and Cindy running around like the hostess at a concert hall, making sure all of her overnight guests had everything they needed, they stood rigidly against the wall.

Dusty approached them. "We could use your help," he said. "We still have a few cots to set up, and we need to clean up the dishes—"

"We're not staying," Hyram said. "We didn't know she had turned this into a wild hoorang when these people are so desperate."

"You know, you're right," Dusty said sarcastically. "These people ought to act depressed. After all, they just lost their homes. The gall of her to cheer them up."

Ellen Hartzell gave him a bitter look. "That isn't what we're saying! Why do you always twist our words?"

"Then what are you saying?" Dusty asked. "Are you praising your daughter for caring about these people enough to give them something of her own? Are you proud of her for reaching out to them or embarrassed because of the way she's reaching out?"

"We're just asking why it has to turn into a fiasco? Why does it have to be a three-ring circus?"

Dusty watched Cindy flitting around, her eyes effervescent and that ever-loving smile still brightening the whole room. She was gorgeous, and her heart was just as beautiful. But her parents would never see what she was, because they were only concerned with what she wasn't.

"When she first told me what she wanted to do," he said, "I thought it was nuts. Now I think it was a world-class idea. People will remember it for years, and you know what? It'll be one of the good things to come out of this storm. At least, that's what Brother Allen said.''

Hyram looked alarmed that his preacher might have anything to do with this, and when Dusty nodded toward him in a group of men setting up the cots and tapping their feet to the music as they worked, Hyram looked appalled.

"Now, if you want to hang around here," Dusty said, "I suggest you either start having fun or start helping. There's a lot of people to feed and bed and a lot of sadness to quell. If you don't have anything to offer, then go home. We don't need you here.''

With that, Dusty walked off, and it wasn't until he looked for them later, and didn't see them, that he realized they'd taken his last suggestion. The richest people in town had gone home to their nice cushy mansion, while their disinherited daughter gave everything she had to people she didn't even know.

BY THE TIME THE BAND quit playing and the "guests" had all settled down for the night, Cindy was exhausted. But strangely, her eyes still glowed with exhilaration as she and Dusty collapsed in her living room.

"Brother Allen said that a lot of these people will be able to go back to their homes tomorrow, since he's organized so many of the men to temporarily patch roofs and stuff. The mayor's having some trailers brought in tomorrow for the rest of them . . . the ones who won't be able to go back for a while . . . or ever.''

"So the planes can sleep in their own beds tomorrow night?" he asked with a smile.

"Yeah." Her smile slid into him, warming him in places he hadn't known existed until she had come along. "Dusty, thanks for helping me with this. You didn't just do it because I insisted, did you? You did want to help, didn't you?"

"Not at first," he admitted. "To tell you the truth, I was more or less a spectator, waiting to see what you'd do next. But then I realized what a great thing it was, and I couldn't help diving in."

"My parents left a check for ten thousand dollars," she said. "I gave it to Brother Allen to decide how best to use it. Wasn't that nice of them?"

Dusty could barely work up a response. "Uh... yeah. I guess it was."

"I think they're coming around. I'm starting to feel like their daughter again."

"Is that a good thing?" he asked.

She smiled. "It's who I am, good or bad. At least I'm not a total outcast anymore. I'm thinking I might even warrant an ungrudging invitation to Sunday dinner next week."

"Is that why you did this tonight? To win the approval of your parents?"

"No," she said, and he knew she meant it. "I quit trying to win their approval years ago. I just want some respect. And a place in their lives again."

Dusty got up and joined her on the couch. His hand stroked her hair as he looked at her, and she smiled. Again, he felt that stirring that he could never ignore when she was around. "I've been giving you and your family a lot of thought," he said. "And I think one of your problems with intimacy is your relationship with them."

Her smile faded, and she laid her head back and closed her eyes. "Oh, no. Not the amateur psychoanalysis. I hate that."

"It isn't that hard to figure out," he said softly, grazing her neck with his knuckles. "Your parents don't want real closeness. They can't share that kind of intimacy. So all your life, you've been trying to do things to get their attention, only it isn't that kind of attention you wanted. You just wanted genuine love."

She opened her eyes and stared up at the ceiling, and for a moment, he thought she might cry. But then she surprised him again, bursting into laughter that she had to muffle with her hand. "That's pretty bad," she said. "If I were you, I'd keep my day job."

He didn't let her flip attitude sway him. "Laugh if you want, but I know it's true," he said. "It's why you have so much trouble getting close to me. You're jam-packed full of emotions and passions, but you're afraid to feel them, because you've been rejected so many times."

Her laughter faded, as did her smile, and finally she brought her eyes up to his. "You're real full of it, you know that?"

"Maybe," he said. "But I think it's true."

"And if it was," she asked, "what would you suggest I do about it?"

"Get close. Allow yourself to have a real relationship."

"You mean, allow you to get me into bed again?"

He stiffened. "Actually, my observation had nothing to do with that."

"Oh, no?"

"No. And if you think it did, then you're the one who's full of it."

He got up and strode across the room. "I'm going now."

"Good," she said. "Don't wake anybody as you leave."

"I'm not leaving," he said. "I'm sleeping on the couch in the office. I don't like leaving you here with all this, so you can call me if you need me. To help you, that is. God forbid you should have any other kinds of needs."

She stared at the door as he closed it behind him, and for a moment she told herself that he had a lot of nerve coming in here and analyzing her that way. But then she realized that there was a great deal of truth to what he'd said. And she supposed that, on some level, she'd known it for a long time.

She dropped onto her bed and closed her eyes, and saw the way he'd touched her, kissed her, held her when they'd made love. It had been so perfect . . . too perfect. Why had she gone and screwed it all up?

She pulled herself off of the bed and went to the front door, cracked it open and looked out over the families sleeping soundly there, after losing so much. Tonight she had met people she'd never known before, and they liked her. Tomorrow, they would know who she was—not some flighty little renegade rich kid who did as she pleased, but a local businesswoman who had helped them when they needed it. Someone who could be counted on—someone who practiced what Brother Allen preached.

She was building her home here, she thought, and it had nothing to do with a house or even a name. It had to do with where she decided to leave her heart. Who she allowed herself to invest it in.

She glanced over at the suitcase, which still lay open on the floor, and, taking a deep breath, she reached into it and pulled out the stack of clothes still there. Quietly, she took it to the bedroom, slid out a drawer and placed the clothes neatly inside.

There, she thought, stepping back. She had unpacked. It had been easy. And the risk didn't seem nearly as great as it had before. She didn't need her parents' approval. She had a home with or without them.

She only wished it would be as easy to unpack her heart and suffer the risk of letting it be broken again.

Chapter Twelve

It was a few days later, after all of the victims had been placed into homes of their own, and the sunshine came out again, that she and Dusty resumed their regular flying schedule.

He was between loads one sunny morning, answering a few phone calls from his farmers, when he heard Cindy's voice over the radio. "Oops."

The lights in the office flickered, and then they went off, casting him in darkness. Frowning, he looked around.

"Uh...Dusty, I have a little problem up here. Would you do me a favor and get out your binoculars and come check to see if I'm on fire anywhere?"

It took less than a second for the significance of her words to sink in, and cursing, he grabbed his binoculars and ran out to the tarmac. Finding her in the sky, he searched her plane. There was no fire, but a long wire hung from her wing.

Going to the radio in his truck, he said, "You're all right, Cindy. No fire. What the hell happened?"

"Uh...I'll tell you when I land," she said. "It's not the kind of thing I want anybody else to hear."

His heart began pounding out of control, and he yelled, "Get the hell down now!"

She didn't answer, but he saw her coming in to land. He waited, breath held, until she was taxiing up the strip.

When the plane stopped, she pulled off her helmet and raised the door. Dusty saw the electrical wire hanging from her wing, and climbing up there, he examined it.

"What in God's name did you do this time?" he asked.

She winced and climbed out of the plane. "I, um...ran through a power line."

"Aw, hell," he said. He jumped off the wing, started inside, then in a rage, flung around. "You're crazy, do you know that? Certifiable! Your parents are right!"

"Dusty, I didn't see it. I don't know this area as well as you."

"Damn right, you don't. Isn't that what I tried to tell you?"

"Where are you going?" she asked.

"Inside to call the electric company," he said. "And find out just how much damage you did."

"Wait!" She caught up with him and grabbed his arm. "Dusty, please. Can't you say you did it? You're allowed to goof every now and then, but I was just making headway with the town. If they hear about this, they'll think I'm as incompetent as they predicted."

"And they'd be pretty much right," he shouted. "Damn it, do you know how dangerous that was, Cindy? You could have been electrocuted. You could have crashed. You could have ruined the plane."

"But I didn't," she said. "The fact is, if I weren't such a good pilot, it would be much worse. I minimized the damage as much as I could."

"Minimized the damage?" he asked. "If that's the line I'm thinking of, it supplies light to half the county."

"Oh, no!" she said. "Dusty, please. Tell them you did it. I'll pay you double this month! Just please—"

"I'm going to tell them exactly what happened," Dusty said through his teeth.

She pushed past him and got to the office door first. "All right, then. I'll call. If I have to take the heat, I'll do it all the way."

She went to the phone and picked it up, muttering as she thumbed through the phone book. "Whatever happened to chivalry, anyway? All I did was cut a stupid wire. It's not like I started a nuclear war."

The absurdity of the whole thing almost seemed funny, but he couldn't quite get amused. "Just make the friggin' call."

"And I didn't even hurt the plane. That's *something*."

"It's under Mississippi Power & Light. Tell them it's the Chandler farm off of Highway 16, between Sartia and Yazoo."

She looked up. "What if I didn't call? Wouldn't they just find it eventually, anyway?"

He gestured around him with outstretched arms. "The electricity is out. You think nobody's gonna notice?"

"Well, they don't have to know I did it!"

"They'll figure it out," he said. "It won't take a genius to realize it was a crop duster plane."

"How will they know which one?"

"Because you're the only one here who just started flying. Unless they're stupid, they'll know immediately who did it."

"Well...maybe they *are* stupid. Maybe they'll think a woodpecker did it or something..."

He raked his hand through his hair and threw up his hands. "Cindy, you're going to give me ulcers. I can't deal with all this."

"Let's not blow it all out of proportion, Dusty. It's a crisis, but not a horrible one." Brooding, she punched out the number for MP&L and did the best tap dance he'd ever heard. "Uh...our electricity seems to be out, and I noticed a wire down, which might be the problem." She gave the location of the power line, then, looking like a kid who'd just escaped a deserved spanking, she hung up. "There. That wasn't so bad."

"Because you lied!" he said. "You think no one's gonna tell them they heard a crop duster flying over there right about the time the lights went out? You think no one heard you say 'oops' on the radio? *Oops,* for God's sake!'' He covered his face, and slowly his shoulders began to shake.

He was laughing, Cindy thought, which meant that things couldn't be quite as bad as he said. No matter what happened, if he could still laugh, she was all right. "Okay," she said on a sigh. "What do you think they'll do to me?"

"Who knows?" he said, wiping his eyes and trying to stop laughing. "Depends on what they find when they get to the site."

She thought for a moment. "Well, maybe I'd better go there, too. See if I can do a little damage control."

"You mean, see if you can flirt your way out?"

"Not flirt, necessarily. Just explain. It might help."

His laughter finally died, and he took a deep breath. "Have a go at it," he said, waving his arm. "It can't get any worse."

She didn't move. "Will you come with me?"

He grinned. "Nope. Somebody has to stay here and field the phone calls."

"Great. Yeah, do that." Lifting her chin, she started out of the hangar. Then, just before she got through the door, she turned back. "If my father calls..."

He waited, bracing himself for the lie she'd concoct. "Yeah?"

He saw the defiance rising to her expression. "Tell him that I single-handedly wiped out the electricity of half of Yazoo County, and I'm proud of it."

He grinned.

"Tell him I'm going after the other half tomorrow." She grinned.

Then, taking a deep breath, she strode out to her car and drove to the scene of the crime.

AN HOUR LATER, when Dusty answered the phone and heard Mrs. Hartzell's voice, he couldn't help smiling.

"This is Ellen Hartzell. Is my daughter there?"

"No, I'm afraid she's not in right now." He heard her car outside and briefly considered covering for her. "Wait . . . she just drove up."

"Is it true what they're saying? That she knocked out the electricity?"

The humor of the whole morning was just beginning to catch up with him, and still grinning, he covered his face. "Uh . . . what exactly did you hear?"

"That she crashed into a pole. Is she all right?"

His smile faded, and irritation surged through him. "If you thought she had crashed, why didn't you ask how she was first?"

"Because everybody says she's all right."

"Everybody? Everybody also said she had crashed, which is a lie."

"So did she knock out the electricity or not?"

He glanced up and saw Cindy in the doorway, looking like a conquering angel in a she-devil suit. She was smiling, but he couldn't seem to return it. "If you're calling to find out when your lights will be back on, Mrs. Hartzell, why don't you call MP&L?"

"Of course that's not why I'm calling! Let me speak to my daughter!"

Compressing his lips, he held the phone up for Cindy to take. "Your mother."

Moaning, she took it from him. "Hi, Mom. What's up?"

"What's up?" she asked. "Cindy, what have you done now?"

Cindy sat down in one of the empty chairs and propped her feet on the desk. "It's a conservation thing, Mom. This county uses entirely too much electricity." Dusty almost spit out the coffee he'd just sipped and covered his mouth to stifle his laughter.

"Cindy, everybody's lights are out. Everybody's!"

"No, not everybody. I hear Tennessee is functioning normally, and most of Alabama is okay."

"Cindy, when are you going to get it through your head that you're not cut out for this before you embarrass us so badly that we're forced to move?"

Cindy's face reddened as she held the phone to her ear, and she rubbed her temple and closed her eyes. "Look, I realize I've made a couple of mistakes, Mom, but these things really are flukes. I didn't mean to hit a line, and the night I got caught in the dark, the worst thing I can be accused of is working too hard."

"Cindy, you're a complete failure at this! Everybody sees it. Everybody is talking about us and about the latest shenanigan our daughter is dragging us through. Don't you see what you're doing?"

"I'm just trying to make a living, Mom."

She met Dusty's eyes, saw that his amusement had faded. He thought she was a wimp, she realized, and it wasn't a role she liked to be caught playing.

"There are easier ways to make a living without making a fool out of yourself, destroying the community and getting yourself killed in the bargain!"

Cindy sighed and closed her eyes. She couldn't let Dusty see her crying. Not again. Not like this. "Uh...I have to go now, Mom. Someone's driving up."

She set the phone back in its cradle and started to make a quick exit, but Dusty came to his feet and blocked her. "You okay?"

"Yeah. Great. I have to go upstairs for a minute...."

"Why don't you want me to see you crying?"

She feigned a smile. "I'm not crying."

"Yes, you are. Look at me."

She looked down at the floor, unable to face him, but he touched her chin and brought her face up to his. For a moment they locked eyes, hers blue and rimmed with tears, his soft and sweet and comforting. "You know what I think of your family?"

"Don't," she whispered.

"I think they're cold, selfish people who don't deserve the energy you put into pleasing them."

A stray tear stole over her lashes and dropped to her cheek. "Dusty, it's me. I've disappointed them. I've been so unpredictable I was predictable. If you knew what I'd put them through..."

"Why do you think you did that?"

"Did what?"

"Ran away, as fast and as hard as you could. Why do you think you did all the things you did? Rebellion, that's why. Because they never have been and never will be the family that you deserve."

"Well, they're all I've got!"

"Then you've got nothing."

More tears escaped, and she glared up at him. "Thanks a lot." She tried to jerk free of him, but he stopped her again.

"I didn't mean to hurt you, Cindy, but I don't understand how you can thumb your nose at everybody else in the world, but you'd give anything just to get one little morsel of approval from them."

"Dusty, this is none of your business."

"No, you're right. It's not." He let her go and stepped back, and she started toward the stairs. But just as she reached them, he caught up with her. "There's something between us, Cindy. Something more than chemistry. A lot more, and that's why this *is* my business."

She seemed to straighten as she swept her hair back from her face. Then she seemed to wilt again. Dusty, unable to maintain his distance, crossed the floor and pulled her against him.

She was like a rag doll in his arms, soft and pliable and vulnerable, and he could feel her shoulders trembling as she cried against his shirt.

But that very vulnerability embarrassed her, and as he might have predicted, she pulled back, wiped her eyes and whispered, "They're not going to report me to the NTSB. They're going to chalk it up to tornado damage. They'll act like it was hanging and didn't break all the way until today."

He smiled down at her. "How did you talk them into that?"

She shrugged. "Charm, I guess. That, and promising to dust the lineman's father's crop for free."

"In other words, you bribed him?"

"I prefer to think of it as a reward. He's doing me a big favor."

Dusty started to laugh, and as he did he dropped his head against her shoulder.

"What's so funny now?"

"You," he said. "No matter what kind of mess you get into, you always seem to land on your feet."

"I do, don't I? If you think about it, I'm a pretty resourceful person. And I haven't endangered anyone's life through all this, so there hasn't been any real harm done."

"Just your own life. But I'm not sure you put a lot of value on that, anyway."

"Oh, that's where you're wrong," she said softly, looking up into his eyes. "I put great value on my life."

"So do I." His gaze locked with hers, and after an eternity, he whispered, "You're the most fascinatingly unusual woman I've ever known."

"Thank you," she whispered.

His lips grazed hers, lightly, sweetly, and when he finally crushed her against him and kissed her with all the passion that had built up in him since the night he'd had her fully, she felt herself surrendering to him and taking him captive at the same time.

"Let's go upstairs," he whispered.

She was just about to consent—he was sure of it—
when she heard the sound of a car outside. Glancing
through the window, she saw her mother's car driving up.

"Oh, no. Looks like we have company."

"Yeah." He sighed and let her go. "Guess I have
some flying to do, anyway."

"Don't leave me here. I need reinforcements."

For a moment longer, they gazed into each other's
eyes, before her mother opened the door. She let go of
him, giving him one last beseeching look. Turning to
her mother, she said, "Hi, Mom. You didn't have to
come over here."

"If I can't finish a conversation with my daughter
on the phone, I have no choice but to finish it face-to-
face."

"Mom, the accident could have happened to anyone. Couldn't it, Dusty?"

Dusty crossed his arms and leaned against the door,
anxious to watch her tap-dance again. "Never happened to me."

Her eyes shot him a *thanks a lot* look. "The lights
will be back on in a day or so. No real harm done."

"Do you have any idea how close you came to
crashing again?" her mother railed. "Look, I've spoken to your father, and we have an offer for you. You
can keep the business. Just let Dusty run it, and we'll
set up a new bank account for you, and you'll never
have to work again."

"Mom, I've made up my mind. This is what I do now."

"But it's too big a risk!"

"Everything's a risk!" She crossed the room and set her hands on her mother's shoulders, but the woman had trouble looking her in the eye. "Don't worry—okay, Mom? I'm not taking any money from you, and I don't want a job, or a place to live, or anything. I'm just fine right here. I made a mistake, but—"

"A mistake? The next mistake might land you in the graveyard, Cindy! Haven't you put us through enough? Don't you know your father and I have nightmares about you falling out of the sky?"

Cindy felt those renegade tears pushing to her eyes. "I'm sorry, Mama. But this is who I am."

"This is who you are *this* week!" her mother spouted back. "It's just a job, for heaven's sake. You can change it as easily as you always used to change countries."

"But you know I'm not doing that anymore, Mama. I came back here to make a home for myself. This is for real, and I'm not giving it up. If you haven't gotten used to the fact that I'll never be a nice little debutante type, you never will. But that's okay. Regardless of how you feel, I'm going to do this."

Her mother's face reddened like the crimson blouse she wore. "I've tried, Cindy. No one can say I haven't tried." Then, pivoting at the door, she slammed it behind her.

Dusty turned back to Cindy. "Why didn't you accept her offer, Cindy? It would have put you back in their good graces. Isn't that what you really wanted?"

"No," she said. "What I want is to be respected for who I am, and loved in spite of it." She sighed. "Besides, I have things to prove to myself. I realize I don't have a real good track record for stick-to-it-ness."

Dusty stepped toward her. "Then maybe you should give it up. You could step back and stop flying, let me run the business, and hire someone to take your plane."

She smiled and shook her head. "No can do."

"Why not?" he asked. "You know I'm going to do what's right for the business."

"And so am I," she said. "Or try to."

Looking bedraggled and weary, he slipped into his jacket. Disappointment tugged at every line on his face, and she knew that he would like nothing more than for her to take her mother's offer. "All right. Whatever you say. I'm going to fly."

He started to walk away, but Cindy stopped him. "Dusty?"

He turned back.

"You can't decide if you like me or not, can you?"

He almost smiled. "As a woman, you drive me to the point of obsession. As a boss, I'm still trying to figure out how to get rid of you."

"Just give me time," she said. "According to my parents, I'll do myself in and you won't have to worry anymore."

Smiling, he left her, and she felt the chill of abandonment, a chill she had felt before. But this time it was temporary, she told herself. He would be back, again and again, because she still had something he wanted very much.

Chapter Thirteen

The fact that the county of Yazoo got its power restored even more quickly than expected did nothing to quell the gossip flying around about Cindy and her airheaded part in the fiasco. Sid Sullivan, always quick to find an advantage, made good use of the wagging tongues. And when he had the nerve to show up at her hangar, Cindy felt her hackles rising.

"Just wanted to let you know I've revoked my offer," he said.

She crossed her arms and leaned in the doorway of her office, blocking him from coming in. "What offer?"

"The offer to buy your business. Your little trial offer to my farmers failed. One by one, they're all making me their choice."

"Because of your lies?" she asked.

He laughed. "Who needs lies when I have you? You've done things I haven't even thought of. It's all real entertaining, little gal, but it doesn't do a lot for them farmers when they need somebody reliable."

She heard the hanger doors sliding shut as Dusty prepared to end the day's work, and after a moment, he strode into the office. With one look at Sid, he asked, "What are you doing here?"

"Just came to see if it showed," Sid said. "Folks are sayin' you're bein' so jerked around by this little piece that you can't remember which end is up."

"Get out," Cindy said, going to open the door. "And if you come onto this property again, I'll have you arrested."

"Not until I talk to Dusty," Sid said, holding his ground. "Looks like you might be needin' a job soon, and me and Gordy decided we could put all our animosity aside and hire you to work for us. Since we'd be inheritin' all your business, anyway, and all. Need somebody to help us keep up with it."

"I have a job," he said.

"Not for long. This little lady is goin' to run this business right into the ground. That is, if she don't run herself into it first."

"The lady said to get out," Dusty said. "I'd listen to her if I were you."

Sid only laughed. "Don't say I didn't extend the hand of friendship and offer you a job. You know, you should make sure she has a will drawn up. Once she kills herself, the business could revert back to you. That is, if there's anything left of it."

Laughing, he went back out to his truck.

Dusty stood still after he left, looking at her with thoughtful eyes. She was beautiful when she was angry, he thought. Her eyes were as sharp and bright as blue diamonds, and her face held a pink coloring all the way up her cheekbones. "There's a lot of truth to what he says, you know. Business is already dropping off."

"Well, it's no worse than it was when I came along."

"Give it time."

"Farmers are fickle when it comes to money," she said. "I'll get them back. I always land on my feet. I'm famous for it."

Sighing, he went to the sink and began to wash his hands. "You know, if we do lose all our business, and we wind up not being able to make it through the season, I really will have to get another job."

"Why?" she asked. "I paid you a lot of money for this business. Use some of it for a while."

"I've spent all of it," he said. "That's why I had to sell. I had bills to pay. The cost of the business just barely covered it all. I'm back to square one, with nothing except what you pay me per load. And those loads are getting fewer and farther between."

"Dusty, trust me," she said. "I promise you we'll get our clients back."

Dusty massaged his forehead. "Put yourself in my place, Cindy. I've been my own boss for fifteen years and had total control over everything. If things got screwed up, I had no one else to blame."

"Then you should thank me. Now you have me to blame."

He tried not to grin, but she knew he was having trouble.

"You know, I'm really hungry," she said, "and for the last few weeks I've been living off of the burgers and pizza of Yazoo City and when I've been entertaining clients, I've been so busy tap-dancing and talking that I didn't eat a bit. I was thinking of driving into Jackson tonight and eating in a nice restaurant, maybe listening to some decent music..."

She saw the gentle smile softening Dusty's lips. "And?" he asked.

"And... although I realize that some of you tough guys like to do the hunting, I'm asking you for a date. Of course, I'd be willing to let you pay if it makes you feel better."

He laughed. "You would, huh?"

"Yes," she said. "And I'd be willing to get dressed up and do my hair, since you're probably sick of seeing me looking like a crop duster."

"Nobody ever gets sick of seeing you, Cindy."

"Then let's do it."

He hesitated for a moment, and she quickly added, "Unless you have a date with your little red-haired friend. But she probably isn't classy enough to be seen in a nice restaurant. You are taking me to a *nice* restaurant, aren't you?"

His grin crept farther across his face. "Looks like it."

"Great," she said, slapping her legs and starting toward the stairs. "I'd love to go with you. Thank you for asking. I'll be ready at seven."

She knew he was watching her as she pranced up the stairs and, smiling, she made the most of it. Just before she reached the door, she turned back and winked.

Dusty was still grinning as she closed herself in her apartment.

IT WAS AMAZING what a good meal and a couple of glasses of wine had done for both their attitudes, Cindy thought. But maybe it wasn't that, after all. Dusty's attitude had seemed drastically altered when he'd come to pick her up.

Apparently, he had a penchant for Victorian fashions. He had looked downright awestruck as she'd walked down the stairs in her high-collared, lacy white blouse and the sleek, black skirt with white lace beneath the hem. Her hair was up in an old-fashioned bun, with tiny wisps tickling her face.

"How do I look?" she'd asked boldly, knowing full well she would have knocked the socks off a blind man.

He smiled. Then swallowed. "Uh...do we have to go out?"

"Darn right."

"Hmm. All right," he said, "let's get this over with."

Smiling, she led him to the car, proud that her efforts had been worth it.

She urged him to take her to Nick's, since it was known to be one of the most expensive restaurants in town, and he lavished her with the best bottle of wine and the best steak in the house.

"This has been wonderful," she told him when they were preparing to leave. "Very romantic."

"Yeah," he said, "but maybe a little too predictable. Anybody could have brought you here. Food is food. Wine is wine. I'm going to take you someplace now that will escalate this to the date of your life."

"I don't know," she said skeptically. "I once went dancing on the Nile. And then there was the hanggliding date where I flew over a mountain range in Spain. Those were pretty exciting dates. What can you do that's better than that?"

He pulled her chair out and brought her to her feet. "I can make you laugh," he said.

He drove her across town, to a place called Brad & Charlie's, and beneath the large neon sign was a smaller sign that read Casino Arcade.

"What is this?" she asked.

Grinning, he found a parking place in the packed parking lot and got out of the car. "You'll see."

She got out, and he took her hand and pulled her into the huge building. People were everywhere, engaged in games she didn't understand. He pulled her through the crowd, found one of the hosts on the floor and handed him some money. The man led them farther in, until she saw a room with a huge video screen on the wall. He turned back to her, grinning. "How do you like video games?" he asked.

She shrugged. "They're okay, I guess."

"Have you ever been *in* one?"

Frowning, she looked up at the screen. "What do you mean?"

The host handed them two suits that looked like something out of *Ghostbusters,* with tanks that strapped onto their backs and big helmets. She grinned as she looked down at them. "What are these for?"

"Put them on, Cindy," Dusty said as he fastened his own on. "And prepare to die."

Still confused, but recognizing the challenge, she began to don her gear. But when she pulled the helmet on, she saw a tiny video screen in front of her eyes, the same screen that covered the whole wall of the Virtual Reality stage. "What is this?" she asked, pulling the helmet back off.

Dusty grinned. "Step into that ring over there," he said, pointing to a circle on the floor. "I'll stand in this one."

She replaced her helmet and did as she was told, and instantly saw her own figure on the screen. "We're in the game?"

"That's right," he said. The host handed her what looked like a machine gun, and Dusty pulled his helmet on. "We're both on the screen as part of the game," he said. "We have to try to kill each other before something else on the screen gets us."

Laughing, she pulled her helmet back on and tried to figure out where she was in relation to the screen. Dusty fired at her, and she ducked. Laughing, she figured out which way to turn to make her character function as she wanted it to, then, pouring every bit of concentration she had into the effort, she set about to snuff him off the screen.

Cindy didn't remember when she'd ever felt so silly or laughed so much. By the time Dusty had killed her three times and she'd killed him once, they were exhausted. Finally, still laughing and panting, they turned their suits over to someone else.

"What was that called?" Cindy asked as they dropped into a booth and sipped on the drinks they'd ordered.

"Virtual Reality," he said. "Fun, isn't it?"

"The most fun," she said. "Even better than hang gliding or dancing on the Nile. Almost as good as flying."

"Which is better than sex—isn't that what you said?"

She grinned and met his eyes. "That was before I'd had it with you." He laughed, and she knew she'd said what he'd wanted to hear.

"You're pretty good at that, you know."

"What? Sex?"

He chuckled and set his drink down. "No. You're damn good at sex. I was referring to Virtual Reality."

"You should tell my parents," she said. "They've told me that I wouldn't know reality if it hit me in the face."

"It did a time or two tonight," he said. "By that fourth game you were a pro. The next time we come, you'll probably cream me. You will come with me again, won't you?"

"Depends," she said. "If no one runs me out of town first." She sipped her drink, looking at him over the rim. "So, Dusty," she said. "What are we going to do about this mess you've gotten us into?"

"The mess *I* got us into?"

She laughed. "Well, I may have had a little something to do with it."

He rubbed his hand across his freshly shaven jaw. "You know, I have been thinking about it. I got an idea on that last game when we looked like choreographed actors in an action movie."

"Really?" she asked, her eyes brightening even further. "What is it?"

He sat back in his chair and grinned at her with mischief in his eyes. "There's an air show coming up in two weeks in Pocahontas. A good friend of mine puts it on."

"Yeah, I've heard about it," she said.

"People come from all over. A lot of the pilots in the state fly in for it. I was thinking..."

"Yeah?"

"We could fly in, too, and if we could work up a few stunts between now and then, you and I could probably do a little show of our own. They're always looking for new stuff."

Her smile sparkled in the sapphire depths of her eyes. "I like it. But do you have enough faith in my flying to do that with me?"

He rubbed his jaw again. "It's the everyday stuff that seems to trip you up. As long as it's daylight and there are no power lines around, we'll be just fine. And if you can crop dust, you can do a few little stunts in the air." He laughed. "If all went well, it could sure clear up our reputations. A lot of our farmers will be there, and those who aren't will hear about it. Wouldn't hurt to give them some kind of reason to think you know what you're doing."

"When do we start practicing?"

"Now that business has dropped off, we have plenty of time. We'll work it in a little each day," he said. "Both of us could be thinking of stunts, and we could choreograph the whole thing."

She took his hand across the table. "You're a genius," she said.

"That's what I've always thought," he said. He squeezed her hand. "Come on. There's one more place I want to take you. Boomers."

"Boomers?" she asked. "Don't tell me. They simulate earthquakes and the survivors get to take over the world."

"No," he said. "It's an oldies club. We're going dancing."

THERE WAS NO BAND at Boomers, just a deejay spinning oldies, but the over-thirty crowd crushed onto the dance floor as if they'd been transported back to the late sixties.

Somewhere, somehow, in the years of his life in Yazoo City, Mississippi, where Cindy was sure he must have been sheltered and smothered from the outside world, Dusty had managed to pick up a few dance steps that put the others to shame. He jitterbugged with the oldest couples in the club, and spun and flipped Cindy as if they'd been dancing together for years. Though she didn't have a clue what he was going to do next or whether she would fall on her face or fall into place, she didn't care. Dusty made everything feel good.

Despite the fact that they had to work the next morning, they stayed until the club closed and they were forced to leave. Then, exhausted and exhilarated, they drove home, quiet, contemplative, content.

It wasn't until they were almost home that Cindy looked over at him. "What are you thinking about?" she asked. "You're awfully quiet."

He didn't look at her. "Well, I'm thinking about what will happen if our stunt at the air show doesn't make business pick up."

She felt it coming, that dreaded right-between-the-eyes honesty. "And what would that be?"

"I think I'd have to quit, Cindy. Try to sign on flying for somebody else, though it might be hard to find a place this late in the season. Especially since I don't own my own plane anymore."

She swallowed as he pulled onto the road leading to the hangar. "Why couldn't you just finish the season?"

"Because," he said, "I get paid by the load, and if we don't have enough business, there won't be enough loads."

She felt tears stinging her eyes, but it made her angry, so she pushed them back. "But if you leave, I might as well close up. You're the only reason any of them is still with us."

He sighed and pulled up to the hangar, let the car idle for a moment. "I know that. And that's why I don't want to leave. But it's a matter of practicalities, and I have to make a living."

"So do I," she said on a whispered laugh. "Despite my parents' insistence that I'll never be able to. I made a great living flying in Australia, you know. I'm not a total incompetent."

He looked over at her, shooting her a look that said she was crazy. "Of course you aren't. You're a fantastic pilot. It's just different being a crop duster. You have all those extra factors to consider. Flying as low as we have to, there are all sorts of obstacles—trees, wires, wind... Just knowing the right height to spray from and the exact amount of wind drift is... Well, it takes a lot of experience. But you've got a real head for it. I have no doubt that you could make this work if—"

"If I didn't keep screwing it up?"

He smiled. "I wasn't gonna say that."

"That's okay," she said. "I know. There's an awful lot of truth in my parents' predictions." She sighed and opened the door, as if about to get out. But she didn't. "You know, I really try not to mess things up. I just love life. I love to get as much as I can out of it. I love to have fun. And I dive headfirst into things that maybe I'm not ready for."

"You were ready to crop-dust," he said. "More ready than anyone else I've ever met who just blew in from training."

"But I get too enthusiastic, and I do stupid things."

"Do you think in fifteen years I haven't had a few mishaps of my own?"

"Maybe because an engine blew or something, but not because you were stupid."

"You aren't stupid," he said adamantly. "And you aren't careless. You're an excellent ag-pilot."

"Not for long. My business is going down faster than an Ag-Cat out of fuel."

"No, it isn't. It's gonna be all right."

She smiled at him, and finally, she said, "Okay, I guess you can stay."

He laughed. "Wait a minute. Have I just been manipulated here?"

"You tell me," she said. "I was just sitting here minding my own business, listening to you extol the virtues of my talent. You talked *me* into keeping you."

He laughed and realized she had effectively turned the conversation around. "I guess the trick is going to be knocking their boots off in the Pocahontas Air Show."

"We will," she said. "You just wait." She leaned her head back on the seat. "You know, something just occurred to me. When I was visiting with all the farmers, I noticed that in almost every house, there was war memorabilia. Medals, pictures, that sort of stuff. If we really want to get their attention, why don't we do some sort of dogfight? You could be the American and I could be the Iraqi, and we could broadcast our radio transmissions over the PA, and make it sound like we're shooting at each other, like in Desert Storm. I'll bet I could get my brother Paul to help.

He's kind of an expert at audio equipment and he knows how to put together sound effects."

Dusty's eyes were distant and contemplative as he tried to picture it. "That could be fascinating. One of us could get shot down and pretend to crash."

"Me," she said. "Let me get shot down. It would be the high spot of the whole show. People all over the county would stand and cheer. Especially my family."

He laughed. "We'll talk more about it tomorrow."

Her smile faded, and she leaned into him. "I feel like a little kid planning some grand scheme that I can never pull off."

"You never had a scheme you couldn't pull off."

"Maybe not," she said. She looked up at him in the darkness, suddenly serious. "I had a wonderful time tonight, Dusty. Thank you."

She saw the poignant seriousness in his own eyes as he looked down at her.

"Even during our worst times, I still seem to have a wonderful time with you." He touched her face, swallowed and grazed her lips with his. "You're a beautiful person, Cindy, and I'm getting real scared at how easy it would be to get used to you."

His kiss was soft, gentle, but its intensity grew as their fires were ignited.

When he broke it, his breathing was heavy. "Why don't I come up with you?"

She closed her eyes and thought how easy it would be to get used to him, too, to learn to count on him, to depend on him, to lose herself in him. And then the heartbreak when it ended would be so profound that she might not survive. Worse, she might not want to survive.

"Not tonight," she whispered.

"Why not?"

"Because I want there to be a tomorrow."

He frowned, not sure what she meant, but she didn't give him time to figure it out. Pressing a kiss on his cheek, she whispered, "Good night."

She left him sitting there, with the car still idling, as she unlocked the door and went into the dark hangar.

DUSTY HAD TROUBLE sleeping that night. There was too much keeping him awake. Too many plans. Too much anxiety. Too much Cindy.

She was getting under his skin in a big way, he thought. It was the first time in his life that a woman had offered him more excitement than flying had. It was the first time one had held his attention for longer than a few days without his having to make a concerted effort not to lose interest. It was the first time he'd dreaded the prospect of not seeing her again.

No, despite what he'd told her, he couldn't quit if things didn't pick up. It wouldn't be possible. Flying would never again be the same without her to spice it up, keep him laughing, keep him worrying. She was an enigma and a free spirit, but she was also a prisoner of whatever fears she held close to her heart. She was a lover, but she was afraid to love. And yet she did it without meaning to. . . .

He closed his eyes and told himself that she had been right about his making a mess tonight. Her words had been facetious, but she didn't know how true they were. She had blown like the wind into a dull and declining existence to bail him out of his own mess, and now he had made it worse by falling in love with her.

Love? he asked himself with a start. Was that what it was? Had he found someone for the first time he could truly love?

It frightened him, it moved him, and it made him want to run as far and as fast as he could. But there was a great part of him that wanted to stay, and a bigger part that feared what he wanted most of all.

Cindy Hartzell, the great thorn in his side, the boss who had changed the face of his business, was all he wanted in the world.

Somehow, he would just have to come to terms with it.

Chapter Fourteen

"It's not going to work." Cindy passed her diagram of their dogfight back to Dusty. "We need at least two more pilots for it to look authentic."

"Yeah, I know." Dusty studied the diagram again. "If it's just us, there's no one for us to talk to on the radio. It takes away a lot of what we had planned."

Cindy lifted her brows and, with a mischievous grin, said, "We could ask Sid and Gordy to join us."

Unamused, he shook his head. "Nah, they'd use real guns." He rubbed his jaw, thinking for a moment. "But you know, I have two real good buddies up in Greenville. Dwight and Billy. They're kind of friendly competitors with each other, but not the blood-and-guts kind like Sid and I are. I'll bet they'd love to do this with us."

"But how would we practice?"

"You and I could maybe chart the whole thing out, and then we could spend the next two Saturdays rehearsing. I'll call them."

He started to pick up the phone when they heard a truck pulling up outside. Looking through the window, Cindy saw her brother Paul getting out.

He was in the door before she had the chance to get up. "Hey, Paul. Thanks for coming."

He smiled and kissed her cheek. "What's goin' on, Sis?"

"We have a favor to ask you," she said. "Something real important, but a lot of fun."

Dusty sat back and watched the various expressions cross over the other man's face. Paul really loved his sister, he thought, just like Dusty had loved his. But Paul was afraid to show it, for fear of having to endure his father's wrath.

"I don't know, Sis," he said. "Dad's laid the law down pretty clearly. We're not supposed to help you until..."

"Until what?" she asked. "Until I capitulate and sell the business? Or until hell freezes over? It's a toss-up as to which could come first."

Paul rolled his eyes and dropped into his chair. "What's the favor, anyway?"

Cindy's eyes brightened as if she hadn't already heard him decline. "We're going to be in an air show," she said, "and we need sound effects for guns and a radio transmission that can play out over the PA. We're doing a dogfight."

"In Pocahontas?" he asked.

"Yes," she said. "Will you help us?"

He frowned and leaned forward, putting his elbows on his knees. "And you're gonna fly in this?"

"Yes. It'll help get my reputation back."

"Back? Sis, you never had one to begin with. You've just reinforced what everyone was already saying."

Dusty didn't miss the hurt passing over her face, a hurt which she quickly pushed away. "Paul, you and I were always the closest. Even though the others were mad at me, I could always see that you still wanted us to be friends."

He sighed. "Cindy, you could get killed."

"No, I couldn't. This is fake. It's a show. I do much worse stuff every day."

Paul covered his face. "Don't remind me."

She sat back, studying her brother. "I'll tell you what. You do me a favor, and I'll do you one. You've always wanted to learn to fly, haven't you?"

He shrugged. "Well, yeah, but there wasn't time. And after you took it up and the family went berserk, I thought maybe I'd better wait awhile."

"In Australia, I gave lessons for a while. I could get my instructor's license renewed, and I could teach you to fly. On your own time, at your own convenience."

"In what?" he asked. "These are one-seaters."

"We'll rent one of the planes at Hawkins Field. No big deal. They rent by the hour."

He sat still for a moment. "Starting when?"

"Right after the show."

"You know, Dad'll have a fit. He and Mom never miss that show. They'll be there, and when they see you up there pretending to shoot at each other . . ."

"They'll finally see what an ace I am. Won't they, Dusty?"

Dusty grinned. "It's gonna be good. It has to be. With your help it can be better."

Paul looked from Dusty to his sister, then back again. "Damn," he said. "I guess I'll do it. The fact is, Dad'll probably be embarrassed enough by you not to even think about what I've done."

"Isn't that the way it's always been?" Cindy asked. "Seems like I just paved the way for all of you. Nobody could ever top me for mischief."

Paul laughed. Then, shaking his head in surrender, he said, "All right. Let's see what you've got, so we can get started."

THE MOMENT CINDY LANDED her plane at the private little airstrip in Pocahontas, she was astounded at the number of people who had turned out for the show. She had no more gotten out of her plane than it was surrounded by would-be pilots checking out this model air tractor and taking pictures, as if it were some rare relic.

She took off her helmet and looked around for Dusty, Dwight and Billy, who had all been at their best when they'd rehearsed last Saturday, but instead her eyes crashed head-on into her parents. Paul was standing there with them, looking a little peevish, as if he dreaded the confrontation when they realized he'd had a part in all this.

Her father gave her a disapproving once-over, taking in her faded jeans and the tight crop-top that clung to her breasts. For a moment, she almost considered jumping back in her plane and flying home to change, but she told herself she was a grown woman and didn't need her father's approval of her clothing.

She heard her name behind her and flung around. Dusty was walking toward her, wearing his usual jeans and tank top, and wreaking the usual havoc on her hormones. His gaze dropped immediately to her shirt, and she saw the admiration in his eyes. She smiled.

"Nice landing," he said.

"It's kind of hard to mess up. Are Dwight and Billy here yet?"

"Yeah. They're over there." He pointed out behind her family, forcing her to look in their direction again.

"Okay. I'll talk to them later. I guess I'd better go offer myself as a living sacrifice to my parents. Let them take their best shots. They don't approve of what I'm wearing, you know."

Dusty grinned and stepped closer to her, the timbre of his voice dropping. "Don't you worry what your parents think. Trust me. That shirt is perfect. As well as what's inside it."

She grinned. "I thought you might think so." She started to walk away but he grabbed her hand and pulled her back.

"You like having men lust after you, don't you?"

She lowered her lids and looked at the moisture glistening on his mouth. "I like having you lust after me."

"Why? You haven't wanted me in your bed in weeks."

She smiled. "That's where you're wrong. I've wanted you every night. I just haven't let it happen."

His smile faded. "Why not, Cindy? What are you afraid of?"

"Worse things than aerial accidents," she whispered. "Trust me. We're doing the right thing."

He saw Sid, half-drunk, staggering toward them, and he let her hand go.

"Hey, Dusty, I hear you and her are gonna be doin' a dogfight. Be better if you just stay on the ground and screw her in public."

Dusty lunged for him, but Cindy stepped between them as Sid swung blindly. "Stop it, Dusty. He's drunk!"

Dusty managed to reach over her head and grab his collar, dragging his face up to his. "You ever talk like that about her again and I'll kill you. Do you hear me?"

He dropped Sid, and the man stumbled back. "Damn, can't take a joke," Sid slurred. "Looks to me like you got a big problem, man. She keeps a short leash and a long whip. How's it feel to have your lover as your boss?"

This time, he scurried away as he spoke, out of Dusty's immediate reach, and Cindy stopped Dusty from going after him. "Dusty, just ignore him. He's trying to get you mad before our show."

"It's working," he said. He jerked his arms out of her grasp and glanced around. Dusty saw that several of the pilots who'd flown in were watching them. What were they thinking? Were they wondering if he'd signed his manhood over to Cindy, along with his business? Were they thinking that she called all the shots? Were they thinking that he had to bow down to her now, just to keep his job?

It was a far cry from last year, when he'd limped to the air show on crutches and been an instant hero for surviving a crash like the one he'd had. He'd been a legend for at least a few hours. Now the story was about how some little blonde had bought out his business, and how he'd been demoted from operator to pilot. They all looked at her, lusting after her and thinking that she had him by the balls or he would have gone to work for someone else weeks ago.

He stepped back, frustrated, and gave her an irritated look. "Go talk to your parents," he said. "I have some people I want to see."

She frowned. "Are you mad at me?"

"No," he snapped. "What would I be mad at? I just want to talk to some of the pilots I only see a couple times a year."

"Couldn't you introduce me? I haven't met any of them."

"You're welcome to make your own introductions," he said. "The less we do to perpetuate this myth that you lead me around by the nose, the better."

Then, without another word, he left her standing there alone.

For a moment, Cindy let the pain of his words wash over her, but then she fought them and lifted her chin, pretending that he hadn't affected her at all. The only thing worse than allowing someone to hurt her, she thought, was letting it happen in public.

To hell with him, she thought. Who needed him?

She watched as he walked into a group of pilots, shaking their hands as if they were long-lost friends. Several looks were tossed her way, and she imagined him talking about how he was still the force behind Webb's Flying Service, and how he was almost to the point of having this little frump straightened out.

Blinking back her tears, she swung around and found her family still staring after her. Her nieces and nephews were piling onto a hay wagon, and her brothers and their wives stood around, all pieces of the whole that compiled her family, looking as if they all belonged.

She was the only one who didn't.

Bopping across the grass to them, she tried to smile. "Hi, Mom. Hi, Dad. What's up?"

Her father's expression, though disapproving, was a little more welcoming than it had been recently. He allowed her to kiss his cheek, then took her shoulders and looked intensely at her. "I just heard that you were doing some kind of stunt today. Tell me it was just a nasty rumor."

She grinned and looked at Paul, who ducked his head. Obviously, he hadn't told them his part in it. "You'll love it, Dad. We're reenacting a Desert Storm dogfight."

"Oh, no." He dropped his hands, slapped them on his thighs, then looked at his wife. "She won't rest until she's crashed, Ellen. It's inevitable."

"Hyram," her mother said. "Forbid her to do it. Don't let it happen!"

Cindy set her hands on her mother's shoulders and gave her a soft, apologetic smile. "Sorry, Mom, but nobody's been able to effectively forbid me to do anything in about ten years. You know that."

"Oh, Cindy, why do you keep doing this to us?" Ellen whined.

Cindy felt that old tension sucking the joy out of her again. "I'm doing it for the business," she said. "We think it'll help. You really don't have to worry. It's all choreographed, and the guns are just sound effects. Lighten up a little. I promise you'll love it. You came here for a show, didn't you?"

"This isn't what we had in mind," Hyram said.

Cindy sighed. "Well, it's going to be great. I have some things to take care of now. Just relax, okay? Have fun."

She started away from them, and her mother stopped her. "Cindy?"

Cindy turned around.

"Be careful, honey. Please."

Cindy smiled and left them standing there. But that look on her mother's face almost made her wish she hadn't come here and given them one more reason to be upset with her. But moreover, she wished she hadn't given Dusty the chance to spit in her face.

Why did she keep setting herself up this way? It was a mystery she had yet to unravel, but no matter how many times people let her down, she still kept expecting more, hoping things would change, wanting things she couldn't have.

She pushed through the crowd, seeing few familiar faces and feeling for the first time since she'd come back to the area that she really didn't belong here. No one cared for her. No one wanted her here. The only reason, in fact, that she'd gotten so attached to Dusty, was that he was forced to accept her. He had no choice. She had confused necessity with emotional attachment.

But the joke was on her.

Tears squeezed out of her eyes and plopped onto her cheek, and she walked faster through the crowd, walking and walking down the rows of parked planes, the food stands, the band playing country-western music.

She walked until she was away from the crush of the crowd, until there was nothing left but grass and a few scattered planes. And then she let those tears fall where no one would see them.

DUSTY SAW HER WALK AWAY from her family, and from the look on her face, he'd had a hunch she was about to cry. Whether it was what he had said or something they had said that caused it, he didn't know.

Excusing himself from his buddies, he started after her, pushing through the crowds of people waiting for the first act to begin.

For a moment he lost sight of her, and he stood still, looking all around him, searching for that deep purple shirt she wore like a model and wondering if he'd blown it for good.

The last thing she'd needed today was for his bruised ego to take retribution on her, he thought. His behavior had been reprehensible. She'd done nothing to deserve it.

Sid had won again.

He raked his hands through his hair and realized that he'd let Sid rile him every time he'd confronted him. That crack about her calling the shots had upset him, but not because of anything she'd done. She had been the dream boss, allowing him to use his judgment in almost every area. With anyone else, it would have been much worse.

He pushed through more people, searching desperately for her, but she was gone.

Damn, he thought, kicking a rock that had the misfortune of lying in his path. What an idiot he'd been. What a jerk!

Slowly, he turned and walked back toward his plane. It would be time for them to take off in just a few minutes, but he wouldn't blame her if she didn't show up. It would serve him right after the way he'd treated her.

Glumly, he made his way back to his plane, wishing he could relive the day, let the whole of the county be damned, and treat her the way a woman like her ought to be treated. Like someone to be cherished. Like the woman he wished he could spend the rest of his life with.

CINDY PULLED HERSELF together and wiped the tears from her eyes when it was time to get back to her plane. Hoping no one could tell that the happy-go-lucky, not-a-care-in-the-world sprite who flew a crop duster for a living had been crying, she pushed back through the crowd to where her air tractor was parked.

She saw Dusty already in his plane, and Dwight and Billy were weaving through people up ahead of her, making their way to theirs. Dusty was watching her, motioning for her to come over, but she pretended she hadn't seen him and averted her eyes as she headed the other way.

She didn't immediately see Sid standing under her plane's nose when she rounded it, but the moment she did, he wobbled toward her.

"Sid, what are you doing here?"

"Just checkin' to see if this baby's in as bad shape now as it was when I was flyin' it."

"It's in perfect shape," she said. "I hope you aren't flying in that condition."

He harrumphed and stepped toward her, staggering. "I can fly in any condition, baby, and don't you forget it. But today me and Gordy drove in."

"Good. I hear the highways are better suited for idiots and drunks than the airways. Just try not to run over any children."

He wheezed. "So you're gonna go up there and take over them airways, are you? Be careful, sweetie. Bad things can happen way up high."

"I can handle it." She pulled her helmet on and pulled herself onto the wing. "Move out of the way, Sid. I'd hate to have to run you over when I pull out."

Grinning and chuckling as if he knew something she didn't, he staggered back to the crowd.

"Cindy." Dusty's voice crackled over the radio, and for a moment she didn't answer.

He didn't deserve an answer, she thought. But that wouldn't work, since it was impossible for them to do a stunt together without speaking. Reluctantly, she answered him. "Come in, Dusty."

"You okay?"

Cindy thought of telling the truth—that she wasn't all right and never would be as long as people she loved found her an embarrassment. But he would know that it wasn't her parents who had shaken her the most, but him. No, she wouldn't give him or any of his friends that kind of satisfaction. "I'm great," she said. "Let's go kick some Iraqi butt."

She looked at him across the tarmac and saw that he was still watching her like a man who knew he'd screwed up but had too much foolish pride to ask forgiveness. It was a curse on the male species, she thought. She'd known it for years but the reality of it continued to shock her. "Let's do it."

He radioed to Dwight, and then Billy, to make sure they were ready to attack. Then, one by one, as another show went on overhead, they took off and scattered until it was their turn.

THE MASTER OF CEREMONIES radioed them when it was time for them to start their show, and Dusty and Cindy fell into a tight formation and buzzed the runway side by side. Pulling up, they watched Billy come in from the east, and the crowd was treated to their scripted radio transmissions.

They played it as if they were Desert Storm heroes flying sorties over Iraq. On the ground far below, the audience could hear their frantic transmissions about enemies on their tails. The sounds of the machine guns added to the excitement, and when Billy pretended to shoot Dusty and he fell off at an alarming rate, Cindy looked below them and saw that every head was turned up, captivated by the show.

She flew down and joined Dusty as he emitted a stream of white smoke, and when he came back up, the dogfight resumed. Together, she and Dusty soared side by side, the sounds of the guns rattling across their radios, as Billy and Dwight pretended to get hit.

After twenty minutes, they had "killed" both of the "Iraqi" pilots, and together, in a last victory stunt, they whipped around in a giant loop, which they had rehearsed until she got it right, and separated at the loop's apex.

When the PA was no longer picking up their transmissions, Dusty radioed her. "Great going, Hartzell. You just changed the opinions of about three hundred people down there."

Cindy whooped and started to radio back, but before she had the chance, she saw something brown trickling across her windshield. It was a few dark drops, like oil, and her eyes darted to her oil gauge. The oil temperature was rising.

"Cindy?"

Deciding not to panic him, she pretended everything was fine. "Yeah, Dusty. Was that great or what?"

"When we get down, I'm gonna buy you a drink. Better yet, I'll buy you a whole case of drinks."

"No, thanks," she said, beginning to smart again from what he had done earlier. "We wouldn't want anyone to get the wrong idea."

More oil splattered onto the windshield, and she caught her breath. She looked out the window, looking for smoke or more splattering oil, but she couldn't see anything.

"Cindy, we need to talk."

Great, she thought. Something to look forward to. Another kiss-off in front of his boisterous friends, if her plane didn't do her in first.

She started to radio back to Dusty about the oil leak, but, frightened that the people on the ground might hear and think she was panicking over nothing, she continued her course around the perimeters of the area, hoping that nothing serious happened before she could make it to the runway.

DUSTY LANDED to a cheering crowd, and as he pulled into the tarmac, he looked behind him to see where Cindy was. There was no sign of her.

He opened his cockpit door, but didn't pull off his helmet, in case she radioed to him before she landed. He watched, grinning, as Billy made it in, then Dwight. The crowd had loved them.

All except for the Hartzells. Already he could see Cindy's father chewing out Paul for his part in the stunt, and her mother was pale, still watching the sky with that wait-till-she-gets-back-down-here look. Cindy would have hell to pay for her victory in the sky, but she always had hell to pay. In fact, Cindy seemed to pay more hell than anyone he knew, for someone who always meant well and enjoyed life as much as she did.

But he was just as bad as her parents. His ego had ruled him today and he had deliberately brushed her off in the interest of being a man. The thought sickened him. He'd had no right to treat her like that when she was his equal in every way. He wouldn't blame her if she headed for home without even landing here.

Finally, as the parachute jumpers piled into their aircraft, he radioed her. "Come in, Cindy. Where are you? Over."

A long time passed before she answered. "Uh . . . Dusty? I have a little problem here."

"A problem?" Alarm surged through him and he sat up, rigid. "What problem?"

"I'm losing oil." Her voice was shaking, something he hadn't heard when she'd been lost in the darkness or had shot through the wire.

"Are you sure?"

"Yes," she said. "There's oil on my windshield, and—" He waited, but she didn't come back on.

"Bring it on in, damn it," he shouted. "Right now! Bring it in, Cindy!"

"The pressure just dropped," she said. "I'm going to have to put it down here..."

"Cindy!" She didn't answer, so he pushed the button again, as if brute force would make her answer him. "Cindy!"

"Oh, God. The engine's locked!"

"Cindy!" Frantic, he looked around and saw that other pilots had heard the transmission and were running toward him. He pulled up until he was leaning out of the cockpit, still wearing his helmet in case of transmission, and scanned the sky for some sight of her.

It wasn't a moment before her father, who had heard the transmission from Paul's radio, was on his wing. "What the hell is going on? Where's my daughter?"

"I don't know," Dusty said. His eyes searched the horizon, out over the tops of the trees, and suddenly he saw a plume of black smoke rising over the treetops. "Oh, my God."

Hyram saw the smoke at the same time, and sucking in a sharp breath, he said, "I've got to get to her."

Her mother screamed, and Dusty shouted, "Does your truck have a radio?"

"Yes!" her father cried.

"Turn it on. I'll radio you where she is when I find her."

He slammed his cockpit door shut and pulled back onto the runway. All the other planes preparing to take off moved out of the way, allowing him clearance.

His hands shook as he took off, and all the while, he tried radioing her again. "Come in, Cindy. Damn it, come in! Now! Cindy, I'm talking to you! Don't do this, Cindy! Damn it, come in!"

Still there was no answer.

He saw the smoke rising bigger and blacker, and as he grew closer, he felt a stark burning in the pit of his stomach. But it was nothing compared to the terror stabbing his heart.

"No," he whispered as he topped the last grove of trees. "No..."

His voice cut off midsound as he saw the yellow wreck engulfed in flames.

Her plane had crashed and it lay crumpled like a piece of foil on the dry, earthy field, and even the cockpit seemed to be melting in the blaze.

"Cindy!" he screamed. His hand trembled as he circled the wreckage, and hot tears burned the rims of his eyes. Trying to steady himself, he radioed Hyram. "I've found her."

"Where?"

He described the field to him and the road that would get him there the quickest, but when her father radioed back, asking if she was all right, he didn't answer.

He couldn't.

The thought suddenly occurred to him that a miracle might have happened, that she might have survived. His crash had looked as bad as this—worse, even. No one had expected him to survive. But his cockpit hadn't been burning....

He blinked the mist out of his eyes and circled around again, determined to land on the same field and taxi as close as he could to her, and maybe get her out of the cockpit before the plane burned completely, just in case she was still alive.

He touched down roughly in the dirt and ground his brakes with all his might. His head told him to stay at least two hundred feet away in case of an explosion, but his heart told him that he couldn't get there faster on foot. Pushing aside his caution, he taxied to seventy-five feet away from her plane. Then, jerking off his helmet, he jumped out of the cockpit and ran as fast as his legs would carry him, then still faster, until he came upon the crumpled body of the plane.

She had gone down practically headfirst, and the nose was bent up, leaving the cockpit smashed. Even if it had been intact, the fire would have eaten her until there was nothing left.

Standing too close to the wreckage, he dropped his head and felt the terror, the tragedy, wash over him. "No!" he shouted. "No!"

"Dusty, get back! You're too close!"

He flung around, and saw Cindy in the trees several yards away, her helmet in her hand and her face smudged with grease and scratches. She was a vision, he thought, a cruel, sweet vision. The most beautiful vision he'd ever seen.

"Oh, God!" he shouted, running across the field toward her and lifting her in his arms. "You're alive! You're alive!"

He swung her around, trembling as he did, and when he put her down, she reached up and touched his face. "You didn't think I was dead, did you?"

He sobbed out a breath and nodded his head.

"Well, any ordinary pilot might be. But I'm no ordinary pilot. I'm Cindy Hartzell, crop duster extraordinaire."

He held her still for what seemed an eternity, just savoring the life left in her, the life he wanted with her. "I don't know what happened, Dusty," she whispered finally. "I did a real careful check before I left our hangar today. Everything was fine, but something happened."

He squinted at the plane, which was still engulfed in flames as the volunteer fire department of Pocahontas rolled onto the scene, sirens blaring.

Turning back to her, he took her face in his hands and whispered, "Cindy, I'm so sorry. For everything. The ego, the anger, the resistance, the lust. I treated you as bad as your family, and as I was looking for you, I kept thinking that it might be too late to tell you. That I might have lost you, and . . ."

"You didn't have to worry," she said, her own voice poignant as she looked up at him. "I had taken Sid's advice. If anything happened to me, the business would have reverted back to you."

Dusty stared down at her, astounded that she thought his feelings were that shallow. "That doesn't matter. Did you honestly think...?"

Before he could finish, her parents' truck screeched to a halt, and several other trucks skidded in behind it. A crowd of people, mostly her family, piled out and began running toward the crash site.

"Before they get here," she said, turning back to him, her face paler than he'd ever seen it, "you should know that I've decided to take them up on their offer." Tears filled her eyes as she went on. "I'm going to be a silent owner of Webb's Flying Service and let you run it. They were right. I guess a competent pilot would have noticed that big of an oil leak. I don't belong in this business."

Dusty gaped at her as her words sank in. "Cindy, you aren't thinking straight."

"Yes, I am," she said. "The crash shook some sense into me, finally. And my mind's made up. In fact, I'll even sell the business back to you when you can afford to buy it back." Her voice cracked and her lips trembled as she tried to smile. "It was a fun experiment, but I know when to quit."

She didn't wait for him to answer as her parents rounded the wreck and spotted her. Slowly, she began to walk toward them.

As if she were their prodigal daughter who'd finally come home, they embraced her and wept with her.

Dusty watched, like the outsider who had been dismissed from her life, the ship that had passed in the night. She had given him everything he'd thought he wanted. Yet, strangely, he felt as though he had nothing.

He watched as she spoke to the firemen. Then, with one parent on each side clinging to her as if she would fall without them, she let them take her home.

Dusty had never felt more alone as Cindy was driven away in her mother's Lincoln, and as she looked out the window at him, he saw the despair, the defeat and the distress in her eyes.

Something more than a crash had happened today, he realized. Even though a miracle had found its way to getting her out of the plane, something in her had died.

He stayed on the site until the fire was put out and the media had shown up to report on what had happened. The wreck was left where it was until the NTSB investigator could fly in to make a report on the crash.

What would they say? he wondered as the last of the stragglers left the scene. Would they blame Cindy for not doing a proper preflight and finding the leak, as she blamed herself?

Dusk swept across the sky, and Dusty knew that he'd better get home before he got caught having to land in the dark as she had once done. But somehow, he didn't want to leave the wreck. There were too many unanswered questions. Too much she was blaming on herself.

He went to the plane, which still smoked where the fire had been put out, and squatted down next to the engine in the nose, which was lying on the ground like a dead animal. The parts were charred, but not burned completely, so he looked at the bottom of the engine. The oil plug wasn't there, and he wondered if it had come out during the crash somehow.

He felt for the safety wire that was there to hold the plug in place, in case it came loose. It, too, was gone.

He ran back to his plane, pulled out a flashlight and hurried back before the darkness could push in all the way. Shining the light to where the oil plug should have been, he saw that the wire had a clean break, as if it had been cut.

That would explain the oil leak, he thought. If the wire had been broken by accident, or cut somehow, the plug might have shaken loose during flight. When if fell out, the pressure would have dropped as all the oil leaked out.

But Cindy would have noticed the broken safety wire before she'd left Yazoo City, wouldn't she?

Not sure what it all meant, he went back to his plane, took off from the bumpy field and headed home.

The hangar was dark and empty when he got back, and he knew she had gone home with her family, rather than to the makeshift home she'd created here. He put the plane in the hangar, then sat in the darkness for what seemed an eternity.

What she'd said before she'd gone to her parents' home, about giving him back the business, should have made him ecstatic. But strangely, he felt as if he'd just had a greater loss than any he'd faced before.

He'd lost Cindy.

He went home and showered, then tried to lie down to rest, but sleep would not come. All he could think of was Cindy's face as she'd told him that she didn't belong in this business. She was incompetent. Her parents were right.

But in his gut, he knew they weren't.

He got up, dressed and headed outside for his truck. It took him ten minutes to reach the Hartzell mansion, and when he knocked on the door, it took ten more minutes for anyone to answer.

Ellen Hartzell didn't appreciate the late visit, but Cindy came down the stairs just as she was about to send him away and told her mother it was all right.

She stepped outside with him, sat on the steps of the house, hugging her knees, and looked up at him.

She looked so small sitting there like that, he thought. One would never know how capable she was. How strong. How smart.

"How are you doing?" he asked softly, sitting down next to her.

"Fine," she said. "I've been counting my blessings. My parents are treating me like a queen."

"Did you tell them what you told me?"

"Yeah," she said. "They were thrilled. I knew they would be." She looked up at him, his face half lit by the porch light. "What about you? Are you happy?"

"No," he said honestly.

She didn't answer, only looked down at her hands.

"Cindy, I stayed on the site until everyone was gone," he said, "and I looked over the engine. Did you know that the safety wire had broken over the oil plug?"

Her eyes shot up to his. "No, it hadn't. I checked it before I left Yazoo. I know it was still intact. I always check to make sure the plugs are tight."

"I thought you did," he said. "And it was a clean break. Not a stress tear. Almost as if it had been cut."

"What?" she asked. "The wire was cut?"

"I'm just saying it looked like it. I can't figure it out, but that's why you lost your oil. The plug vibrated loose during the flight, and it fell out because the wire wasn't there to hold it in."

Her hands came to her face, and she stared out into the night, trying to imagine how it could have happened. "Someone must have done something. They must have cut it, because I'm telling you, it was intact. It wasn't even weak."

"But if you're sure it was okay in Yazoo City, it would have to have been cut in Pocahontas. And who would have tampered with it in front of that crowd? Why would they want to?"

Slowly her face changed, and she sat up straight, bringing her hands down to his arm. "Oh my God. It was Sid."

"What?"

"Sid was at the plane just before I took off. I caught him hanging around under my engine, drunk as a skunk."

"Do you think he loosened the plug and cut the wire?"

"He could have," she said. "It's such a simple thing, probably no one would have seen him. And even if they did, he was too drunk to care. We know he didn't want us to do the act. But did he not want it bad enough to see me dead?"

Dusty shook his head. "I can't imagine it. Maybe he thought you'd just get a leak and have to land before the show. To make you look stupid or scared or something."

She shook her head. "Someone must have seen him. There were people all over the place."

"But everybody was checking out the planes. If he'd reached up with a pair of pliers, chances are that no one would have thought anything of it. The engine's exposed plain as day. Anybody could do that."

"Maybe there was a witness," she said. "Maybe we could find someone who saw him."

Dusty stood up and started down the stairs.

"Where are you going?"

"To visit the sheriff," he said. "Somebody's going to be at Sid's house before he has time to sober up. And if he did anything to that plane, we're going to find out."

"Wait!" she shouted, before he had reached his car. "I'm coming with you."

DUSTY AND CINDY FOLLOWED the sheriff to Sid's trailer and watched from their car as the sheriff and two deputies banged for Sid to open up. It was Gordy who opened the door, and he was shoved back as the men clambered in.

No more than five minutes later, Sid stumbled out in handcuffs.

Dusty and Cindy both got out of the car. "What's going on, Will?" Dusty asked the sheriff.

"He was passed out on the couch in the same puked-up clothes he was wearing at the air show," the sheriff said. "And look what we found in his pocket."

He held up the pair of needle-nose pliers, and Cindy wilted against the car. That thin thread of civility that had held Dusty this far, snapped, and bolting forward, he grabbed Sid's collar. "What were you trying to do to her, you bastard!" he shouted. "I ought to kill you myself and make sure it's done right!"

Sid's head bobbed as the sheriff's men pulled Dusty off and held him back as Sid was led to the car.

"I wasn't tryin' to kill her," he slobbered. "I figured she'd put the plane down before the show. I didn't count on her flyin' in flips before she noticed the leak! It ain't my fault she waited too long to put it down."

Cindy stared at him, awestruck by his stupidity and his skewed logic about the whole incident. Then she realized that what he'd just said was tantamount to a confession. Sid Sullivan was going to jail.

She reached for Dusty, who still trembled with unsated rage and stared at Sid as if he'd tear his head off his shoulders the moment he got the chance. As they loaded the drunken crop duster in the sheriff's car, she leaned tiredly against the side of Dusty's truck bed.

For a moment after the car had driven away, followed by Gordy in his old pick-up, neither of them said a word. Finally, as Dusty's anger slowly drained away, Dusty laid his shaking hand on her back. "Still glad you came back to Yazoo City?"

Cindy lifted her head. "Well, it hasn't been boring, that's for sure."

Dusty pulled her to the hood of his truck, held her waist and lifted her onto it. His eyes were serious and misty red and he gazed up into her eyes. "Now that you know you aren't incompetent, that nothing your parents have predicted is true, that you're really a crop duster extraordinaire, and that you've only added a new chapter to what had already become a legend, will you please reconsider and not leave the business?"

Tears shimmered in her eyes, and she shrugged. "I have to now. I told my parents. I conceded defeat. My mother's fixing up my old room, and she's going to nominate me for entrance into the Junior League."

"You've got to be kidding."

She smiled, but there wasn't much life left in it. "I wish I were."

"Cindy, that'll kill you faster than flying will."

"It doesn't matter," she said. "We only have one plane now. You should be the one to fly it."

"I have a feeling Sid'll be selling out real soon," Dusty said. "Besides, the insurance money will cover the plane. You'll have to buy a new one, anyway."

"*You'll* have to buy a new one," she said. "I'm leaving it all up to you. Silent owner, remember?"

"I don't like you silent."

"Wow. Now there's a confession I'll bet you'll regret one day."

"I hope so." He set his hands on her knees, and his face grew intense with unspoken words. "Cindy..."

"Dusty, it's okay. Really. I'm fine with this."

"No, just listen," he said. He took a deep breath and tried to choose his words carefully. "I was awful to you at the air show today. I acted like a kid who cared more about what his friends thought than about the woman he loved."

Even in the darkness, he could see her cheeks reddening. "Oh, now, I wouldn't go that far...."

"I would," he said. "I've know it for a while now, Cindy. But you held me at such arm's length. But no matter how crazy you've made me, or frustrated, or anxious, I can't get past the simple truth that for the first time in my life, I'm in love."

She sat motionless, watching him, unable to say a word.

"But I've been so wrapped up in my ego, and all I felt I'd lost, that I didn't stop to think how empty my life would be if I ever lost you."

He watched her eyes fill with tears, and he stroked one away, then slid his hand back through the silky length of her hair.

"I'm in love with you, Cindy, and I won't rest until I've made you my wife. I'll write it across the sky, I'll buzz your parents' house twenty times a day, I'll defoliate their rosebushes. I'll do whatever it takes, but I can't live without you.''

She sucked in a sob and slipped down from the hood of the truck, putting some distance between them. ''You're crazy, you know that?'' she asked, turning her back to him.

''Absolutely. Certifiable. You're the only one who can cure me.''

''Cure you? I'm the one who made you that way.''

''Then, as I see it, it's your responsibility to help me.''

''And marrying you is what it would take?''

''Damn right.''

He watched her wipe her eyes, then she turned back to him. ''Dusty, you're the most exciting man I've ever met, and I've been in love with you since that first time you kissed me. But I also understand the realities of a relationship with a man like you, who lives on adrenaline. Who sees the impossible as one thing yet to conquer. You're the kind of man I always want to choose, but you're also the kind that can't be held. There's always another frontier, another battle, another woman....''

''Do you honestly think I'd stand here after you've promised to give my business back, and cook up a deal where we're partners for life, if I had any intention of moving on the minute you're mine?''

Her hands trembled as she turned back to him. ''I'm not going to fly anymore, Dusty, and I'm never getting married again.''

He crossed the grass to her and took her shoulders, forcing her to look up at him. "The love of flying is in your blood, Cindy, and you can't give it up because of a crash, or because your parents made some glum prediction you think came true. You're going to get back up there, baby, and you're going to be my partner. And you're also going to love again, because no matter what your pretty little head tells you, that passion I've already tasted in you is as rampant as the adrenaline that makes you tick. You can't live without it any more than I can. And you know it."

She tried to cover her face, to block out the turmoil catching her in its grip. "I came here to do something," she said. "All I wanted was to—"

"Prove yourself to your parents," he said. "Find a sense of belonging. Make your way in your own way. You did all those things, Cindy. Every last one of them. The world is yours."

"It's not mine," she shouted, shaking out of his arms. "I'm so confused."

His own face reddened as he felt the frustration of seeing everything in perfect clarity while she saw only a blur. She turned back to him, staring at him like a vision that was about to slip away. "This is the moment both our lives have come down to, Cindy. You can either trust me to make you happy for the rest of your life, or you can cling to your fears like a damnable Hartzell and lock yourself back in their expensive prison."

Still, she hesitated, looking at him as if he'd ruined her life by giving her a choice she hadn't the energy to make.

"If it's me," he said, his voice suddenly hoarse, "then I understand. If you're not in love with me, if you don't want to marry me... I'll have to deal with that. But don't walk out on the business," he said. "It's yours. It's nothing to me unless you're a part of it."

He didn't know which part of what he said had gotten to her, but suddenly her face relaxed, and a serenity like he had never seen in her washed over it. "All I know, baby," he whispered, "is that the only thing standing between me and perfect happiness is the three feet of dirt separating us right now."

Before he could catch his breath, she had covered that distance and thrown her arms around him. He fell back against the truck as her mouth found his, and something ignited deep in his soul as he felt her answer.

"Yes, Dusty," she sobbed against his lips. "I'll marry you."

Closing his arms around her, he lifted her off the ground, and in that moment, as the world seemed to spin around them, he told himself that he would never let her go again.

CINDY'S IDEA of a perfect wedding was a barbecue with a live band and a party that outdid the tornado bash she'd thrown. Despite her mother's martyred protests over the whole affair, she arranged a great caterer and smiled through it all.

Every farmer in town was invited to the wedding celebration. Sid was awaiting trial, and after plea-bargaining down to some crime that would probably get him nothing more than probation, he'd still been forced to sell his planes since all his customers had opted to work with an honest couple of legends rather than the likes of the Sullivan brothers.

They got married on the airstrip, and after Brother Allen pronounced them husband and wife, a forma-tion of crop dusters flew over them, saluting the woman who had now earned her place among their ranks.

And as Dusty took her in his arms and gave her the kind of kiss that Yazoo City would buzz about for years to come, Cindy knew that she had finally found her way home.

Take 4 bestselling love stories FREE

Plus get a FREE surprise gift!

Special Limited-time Offer

Mail to Harlequin Reader Service®

> P.O. Box 609
> Fort Erie, Ontario
> L2A 5X3

YES! Please send me 4 free Harlequin American Romance® novels and my free surprise gift. Then send me 4 brand-new novels every month, which I will receive months before they appear in bookstores. Bill me at the low price of $2.96 each plus 25¢ delivery and GST. That's the complete price and—compared to the cover prices of $3.50 each—quite a bargain! I understand that accepting the books and gift places me under no obligation ever to buy any books. I can always return a shipment and cancel at any time. Even if I never buy another book from Harlequin, the 4 free books and the surprise gift are mine to keep forever.

354 BPA AJJQ

Name _____ (PLEASE PRINT)

Address _____ Apt. No. _____

City _____ Province _____ Postal Code _____

This offer is limited to one order per household and not valid to present Harlequin American Romance® subscribers. *Terms and prices are subject to change without notice.
Canadian residents will be charged applicable provincial taxes and GST.

CAMER-93R   ©1990 Harlequin Enterprises Limited

HARLEQUIN CELEBRATES
THE SEASON OF SHARING
AND FAMILY WITH

Friends, Families, Lovers

Harlequin introduces the latest member in its family of
seasonal collections. Following in the footsteps of the popular
My Valentine, Just Married and *Harlequin Historical Christmas
Stories*, we are proud to present FRIENDS, FAMILIES,
LOVERS. A collection of three new contemporary romance
stories about America at its best, about welcoming others into
the circle of love.... Stories to warm your heart...

By three leading romance authors:

KATHLEEN EAGLE
SANDRA KITT
RUTH JEAN DALE

Available in October, wherever
Harlequin books are sold.

1993 Keepsake

CHRISTMAS

Stories

Capture the spirit and romance of Christmas with KEEPSAKE CHRISTMAS STORIES, a collection of three stories by favorite historical authors. The perfect Christmas gift!

Don't miss these heartwarming stories, available in November wherever Harlequin books are sold:

ONCE UPON A CHRISTMAS by Curtiss Ann Matlock
A FAIRYTALE SEASON by Marianne Willman
TIDINGS OF JOY by Victoria Pade

ADD A TOUCH OF ROMANCE TO YOUR HOLIDAY SEASON WITH KEEPSAKE CHRISTMAS STORIES!

AMERICAN ROMANCE INVITES YOU TO CELEBRATE
A DECADE OF SUCCESS....

It's a year of celebration for American Romance, as we commemorate a milestone achievement—ten years of bringing you the kinds of romance novels you want to read, by the authors you've come to love.

And to help celebrate, Harlequin American Romance has a gift for you! A limited hardcover collection of two of Harlequin American Romance's most popular earlier titles, written by two of your favorite authors:

ANNE STUART—*Partners in Crime*
BARBARA BRETTON—*Playing for Time*

This unique collection will not be available in retail stores and is only available through this exclusive offer.

Send your name, address, zip or postal code, along with six original proof-of-purchase coupons from any Harlequin American Romance novel published in August, September or October 1993, plus $3.00 for postage and handling (check or money order—please do not send cash), payable to Harlequin Books, to:

In the U.S.

American Romance 10th Anniversary
Harlequin Books
P.O. Box 9057
Buffalo, NY 14269-9057

In Canada

American Romance 10th Anniversary
Harlequin Books
P.O. Box 622
Fort Erie, Ontario
L2A 5X3

(Please allow 4-6 weeks for delivery. Hurry! Quantities are limited. Offer expires November 30, 1993.)

HARLEQUIN AMERICAN ROMANCE   A10-POP
10TH ANNIVERSARY
ONE PROOF-OF-PURCHASE   092-KBA